"This book is so amazing, and I can't put my phone down. Thank you for writing this."

"I just LOVE reading RED. Good job, keep it up and the ending was totally unpredictable. It's one of my favorite books ever. Keep writing, especially a sequel or a prequel."

"Your book is incredible!! I read it in a couple hours and couldn't put my phone down! You are amazing."

"Your book is so amazing, I read it all in one night. Can't wait for the chapters! Keep up the good work!"

"I am absolutely in love with this book."

Read what some of the other readers had to say at bit.ly/ReadRED

RED

WELCOME TO FAYETTEVILLE

A NOVEL

Wesley Bryant

This book is a work of fiction. Any references to historical events, real people, or real places are used fictitiously. Other names, characters, places, and events are products of the author's imagination. Any resemblance to actual events or people are entirely coincidental. Online promotional contests, with a reward of being featured in the novel, is an exception to the previous statement.

For information on buying in bulk at a discounted price, email the author at wbryant1@harding.edu

Book cover design by Wesley Bryant

Originally published on Wattpad.com beginning in April 2017

ISBN:1717469116

ISBN-13: 9781717469113

First Edition

RED: WELCOME TO FAYETTEVILLE

To Nanny and Papa,

For your never-ending support

"They'll talk about us and discover

How we kissed and killed each other"

—Lorde, *Melodrama*

PROLOGUE

Derrick walked under the neon lights of the small-town movie theater. He reached down and made a risky move: holding Kathrine's hand on the first date. His sharp edge of a jawline emerged from the opening of his dark blue hoodie; he didn't want anyone to see him. Kathrine was willingly holding his hand even though she didn't know exactly *who* Derrick Colten was. She had just moved into town two weeks ago and was glad to be making friends. She was worried that moving at this stage in high school would ruin every dream she ever had. But with Derrick, she liked the way he looked, the way he talked. She felt like it was somehow a reminder of home. "Maybe this could be more," she thought.

The only thing on her mind was Derrick. Because in this moment, all she knew was that he was warm. His hands weren't rough as he rubbed her thumb with his. It felt right... but it wasn't. Derrick had Kathrine blocked on all social media and told her he didn't have it. He didn't want Kathrine to see all of his pictures with Natalie. Kathrine was the blonde that Derrick always wanted, not for a relationship but for a night.

Kathrine Woods was a gorgeous girl. Blue eyes. Full lips. Like most girls, she didn't need makeup, but she still liked it. She had even considered starting a makeup blog. At the least, she would always keep lipgloss on. Her height was just under six foot, just short of Derrick's six foot, 3 inches. She always wore a hand full of simple rings and made sure her white converse shoes matched everything.

Derrick always wore the most recent solid-black, trending tennis shoes with khaki joggers. He was flat-chested and long-legged. He kept his face clean-shaven and showed his dimpled smile. His short brown hair matched his hazel eyes and bushy eyebrows.

Derrick took Kathrine behind the green restaurant on the top of the hill where he had parked his car. He got into the driver's seat; she got into the passenger seat, but not for long. Kathrine was attracted to Derrick, but she wasn't *that* girl. She had caught onto at least one thing about Derrick: he wanted something she wasn't going to give.

He was cheating on Natalie and Kathrine had no idea. She also had no idea what other secrets were in this town. This new small town was full of surprises, and she would be one of them.

1

Natalie tossed her beautiful painting into the trash can that sat in the corner of her room. For some reason, she couldn't see the masterpiece that it was or the talent she put onto the canvas.

Natalie's talent and beauty were the same: natural. Her short brown hair was wavy, and she *hated* it. Her eyes were cotton-candy blue, which just so happened to be her favorite color. She was short and petite in size, but she wasn't boney. Her favorite outfit was simple: leggings and an oversized t-shirt (probably Derrick's), but she could only wear it when she wasn't at school. Good thing it was Christmas break.

The green and blue watercolors dripped from the canvas to the wrapping paper in the trash can. It was the leftovers from her present she got Derrick Colten, her boyfriend.

Natalie had wrapped his new phone case in a beautiful, bright red wrapping paper. She felt like the intensity of the color showed how much she loved him.

She flopped onto her bed, grabbing her phone from the white nightstand. Her fingers had dried blue and green paint making her fingerprints show. She scrolled onto Instagram and looked through Derrick's photos, reading every caption.

She loved to look at them. It was a way for her to relive the great times she had with him. She stopped at her favorite photo he had posted. It was a moment she would never forget, standing on a bridge watching the fireworks show over the rippling water.

That's why she loved her best friend Jasper. He was great! But he took even better photos. She would let him snap photos of her and Derrick every time they were together.

I love this one she typed to Jasper after sending him the Fourth of July photo he took.

Thanks! How are you? he responded.

...I'm okay.

What's wrong?

I just miss Derrick. I know that's annoying.

No, it's okay lol. Where is he?

10

He's at home asleep.

And Natalie believed it... She really believed that Derrick was asleep. She had not even considered that he was making out with the new girl, Kathrine, in his car just five minutes from her house. Derrick had both of the girls fooled. Neither girl knew about the other. But that's the way things go. People like Derrick stay in control until someone talks. And in a town like Fayetteville… people talk.

"That's weird. All these white cars?" Genni laughed, pointing in the dimly-lit store parking lot.

Genni was short, so Kathrine towered over her. Her real name was Genesis, but "Genni" got less attention. She laughed a lot, which showed off her bleach-white teeth. Her cheeks were plump, and freckles danced on her nose.

They knew they probably shouldn't be there, but Genni loved adventure, and she was taking this opportunity to get to know Kathrine. Genni needed to show her that Fayetteville isn't horrible. To show her that this could be home if she would let it be.

There wasn't any wind that night, so their hefty jackets were enough to keep them warm. They couldn't even see their breath—maybe because it was too dark—but it wasn't even cold enough for them to shiver. Occasionally, they'd hear a car driving down Park City hill, but it wasn't close enough for the headlights to even shine on the parking lot. The sparse security lights would have to do.

"What are we even doing here?" Kathrine asked, scratching her arm with her light-orange nails.

"I've never really been over here. I always just pass it going down Park City hill. Who knows what's over here," Ginni shrugged.

"I'm starting to get a little cold."

"Yeah, well, not everyone is used to the beach in Florida," Genni laughed as she kicked a can and let it roll off the pavement of the parking lot and into the dead grass.

"So… you know Derrick, right?" Kathrine asked.

"I don't know if it's a good thing, but yeah… what about him?" Genni asked as she peeked into the window of the rotting store that used to sell farming supplies.

"I think we're a thing… We made out last night."

12

"You did what?!" Genni snapped around to Kathrine so fast she almost lost her balance.

Kathrine leaned back, giving her a confused look.

"Made out? Is that weird?" Kathrine's voice started to shake with uncertainty.

Genni pointed at Kathrine wondering if she was kidding. Genni let her mouth drop, making Kathrine feel uneasy.

"What?" Kathrine asked with wide eyes.

"Oh, wow. He is cheating on Natalie," Genni said to herself, looking up at the night sky in shock.

"He's cheating!?" Kathrine yelled.

"Girl, look." Genni pulled out her phone and scrolled through his Instagram to show Kathrine the truth.

They were both so invested in Derrick's Instagram pictures that they didn't notice the slight sound of the can being stepped on at the edge of the parking lot. Kathrine had her hand over her mouth as they scrolled two months deep in Derrick's Instagram.

Kathrine could just feel it. That feeling when you know you're not alone. Usually, it's just paranoia and you're wrong... but Kathrine was right. They weren't just being watched, they were prey. She felt like a poor animal sitting alone in the parking lot just waiting to be eaten. She listened to her gut and turned around to see the shadowy figure and a red hoodie hiding their face.

"Um, Genni. I don't like this." She nudged her.

"Me either! I can't believe he is cheating."

"No. Not Derrick." Kathrine's voice was trembling as she took a step back.

Genni finally turned around and locked her eyes on the heavy crowbar. The security lights were weak, but she could still see the crowbar too clearly. She couldn't look away from it.

The red hoodie ruffled as the crowbar swung back and forth. Back and forth. The moonlight occasionally catching it.

"*Run*!" Kathrine yelled as she kicked up dust with her heels.

Genni dropped her phone, and the screen shattered on a pebble. She spun on her heels to follow Kathrine into the dark street... but it was too late.

Thud.

Genni hit the pavement of the shady parking lot she knew she shouldn't have been at. Kathrine kept running, knowing Genni was no longer following her.

Then, the killer jerked the crowbar out of Genni's neck, letting her blood paint the white cars red.

2

Kathrine's Converse slapped the road as she ran down Park City hill. She was hoping that someone would stop to help her. She wasn't yelling; she didn't think anyone would be there to hear her. The breeze picked up, but she didn't notice. Her hair wrapped around her face, and she still kept running. Her ankles were starting to hurt from the lack of support in her shoes. She kept running and running down the hill and toward the strip of town. Only the streetlights were on... store signs were off, the usual "nightlife" had gone to sleep. She just hoped she wasn't alone.

The sound of an engine was starting to rumble behind her. She turned her head, letting the breeze flip the hair away from her face. There was only one set of headlights coming down the street. Her stomach was still turning on the inside. She didn't know who was driving. What if it was the same person after her? She didn't really have a choice. She had to trust someone, so she hustled from the turning lane to stand on the right side of the road. The street lights were reflecting off the jet-black car as it started to slow down. The tires rolled to a halt in the middle of the vacant highway. Finally, there was a standstill. She threw caution to the wind and ran to the driver-side door.

Bang. Bang. Bang.

The teenaged girl cracked the window just enough to hear Kathrine's begging.

"Please help me! My friend back there, I don't know what's happening. I was scared, and I ran. I'm new here and I don't..." It was too much for Kathrine to handle. She was flustered and couldn't gather the words she wanted to say.

"Chill, girl. What's going on?" the girl asked from behind the lowered window.

Kathrine made eye contact with the driver. Her chest was moving up and down quickly. "I need... a ride... to the... police station," she uttered between the breaths.

"Is it really *that* serious?"

"*Please!*" Kathrine banged on the window. It made the driver flinch like a jump scare in a horror film.

The driver tapped the steering wheel with her nails as she contemplated what to do. "Don't you have a phone?" the driver asked. She was actually getting angry that she was hitting her car like that.

"Yes. It's dead. I'm scared... please," Kathrine said one last time.

The driver reached across the passenger seat and pulled the locking lever up.

Click.

"Get in." She rolled the window back up the one inch.

Kathrine raced around the car and jumped in the passenger seat. She thought it was strange that no other cars were coming down the street. Yeah, it was midnight, but she was used to busy streets in Florida. In fact, going out late at night alone was something she had never really done. And she doesn't think she would ever do it again.

"What's your name?" the driver asked.

"Kathrine Woods. Thank you for doing this." Kathrine couldn't keep her eyes off the road in front of her. She couldn't turn to the girl. She was thankful, but you couldn't hear it in her voice. She was still trying to catch her breath.

"And don't you want to go back and check on your friend?"

"The cops will be able to do more than I can. I don't know what I'm doing!" Kathrine finished her sentence by yelling. Her breathing was starting to pick up again, and the driver was getting anxious now. She didn't know how to help, so she tried to connect with her as she drove into town and towards the police station.

"Well, my name's Evelyn," she said, still keeping her eyes on the road. "Evelyn Harper."

Kathrine didn't say anything. She continued to stare out the window, bouncing her knee to try to relieve her anxiety that wasn't going away. Evelyn's car smelt like Taco Bell. An empty bottle of Diet Mountain Dew rolled in the back seat. Her bookbag was still in the floor from the last day of school before Christmas break.

Evelyn pulled into the police station parking lot, and Kathrine pulled the locking lever up, and within a second, she was out of the car. She bolted up the cold concrete steps to the glass door.

"Hello?!" she yelled, searching around the door for a way inside. She alternated between yanking at the locked door and banging on it with her fist.

"There she goes again with that banging," Evelyn said to herself. She shut her door and leaned back with her arms crossed. She still wasn't sure what happened, but she thought Kathrine was overreacting.

"Yes?" a voice said from a speaker to the left of the glass door.

"I need help! Someone was after me and my friend in a parking lot, and I ran. I don't know what happened but..."

A deputy opened the glass door from inside, keeping one hand close to her gun. "Ma'am, you need to calm down. Take a deep breath... and we will go inside." Kathrine nodded and followed her lead. The deputy caught a glance of Evelyn leaning against her car. "Can I help you?"

"I'm the ride. I don't know what's going on... I'm fine," Evelyn answered.

The deputy nodded and shut the door behind them.

3

Evelyn looked around the parking lot of the police station. The darkness was intruded by a few floodlights from the station. The chilly breeze brushed her thin black hair to tickle her nose. Her eyes were closer together than most, and she had blushing cheeks.

She was a tough girl, but something about the darkness and being alone was getting to her, even if she was at the police station. She wanted company, but she didn't want to deal with whatever was going on inside the station with that new girl, Kathrine.

Evelyn opened her car door and grabbed her phone from the cup holder below the radio. She unlocked it and called her new step-brother, Zach.

Zach and Evelyn had been friends for years, but now they weren't just friends. Zach's dad and Evelyn's mom had "fallen in love" (so they said) and got married.

"Hey, I know it's late. Don't freak out... but I'm at the police station, and I kinda need you to come here."

"What did you do?" Zach asked, a little pissed off.

"Nothing! Really. I ran into this girl... Kathrine, I think was her name. She's a new girl in town. She was going crazy in the middle of the street and needed a ride here so I brought her. I don't want to ditch her so I'm staying, but I would just like for you to be here."

"Okay. I'm coming." He didn't think twice.

"Thank you," Evelyn said as she ended the call.

Inside, Kathrine was giving her statement to the sheriff himself, Jimmy Mullins. He was in working later than he should, but he was just doing his job. He was large in build and had the strength to match it. He was comforting in the way he talked to the people of Fayetteville. His voice was deep and so was his way of thinking.

"I know it sounds crazy, and I don't know what happened. It was just wrong. My friend Genni... who knows where she is..." she looked up from the desk to Sheriff Mullins, "I'm terrified for her." She had an urgency in her voice.

Sheriff Mullins grabbed the radio. "We're going to head out here and check everything. It's at that old farming store over at Park City hill."

Kathrine felt better, but it wasn't enough to calm her. Yes, she felt safe, but she wasn't anywhere near comfortable. She was proud of herself for running... but her stomach was hurting. Her heart was sinking because she left Genni behind...

Outside, she walked down to Evelyn, confused about the new guy standing next to her. She shot an awkward smile to Evelyn. She was trying to say *This is weird. Who is this? ...* Evelyn got the message.

"Uh, this is Kathrine, and this is Zach, my step-brother." Zach had a massive beard, and he was about the same height as his step-sister.

Evelyn leaned forward. "Listen... our parents are out of town on their honeymoon for the next two or three weeks... I don't know, they don't talk to us—"

"I think it's three weeks." Zach rolled his eyes.

"Well, our house is empty if you wanna swing by and stay the night," Evelyn said.

"Umm, no it's fine. I want to go home and be with my mom... she's on her way," she said as she leaned against the car.

❖ ❖ ❖

Sheriff Mullins pulled into the dark parking lot. As his car turned, the headlights shined on several things: the broken street light, the graffitied walls of the store, then the white cars that had been painted a new color... but it wasn't paint. He grabbed his radio and let his deputies know. He parked his car and stepped outside. He could smell the iron and the stench of blood splattered on the cars.

Sheriff Mullins walked around the parking lot in full alert. He had his pistol in his right hand and the flashlight in his left fist, letting the gun rest on his wrist. He searched the entire parking lot to make sure it was safe. The glass of the building was solid. The door was still boarded shut.

There didn't seem to be anyone here... no killer... *and no dead body.*

4

That night, Kathrine went home to her mom. The anxiety had finally started to let go of her. Her hands weren't shaking as much. Her voice wasn't trembling as much. She ran into her arms. She needed a hug to actually feel safe for the first time in hours. They cried together. They worried together. But at least they were with each other. Kathrine was off to a rough start here in Fayetteville, and she wanted to go back to Florida... but there were bigger problems there.

By morning, everyone in Fayetteville would know some version of what happened that night. Genni's parents were terrified and posting on Facebook, hoping that someone would know something. And when the police told them what they discovered, they didn't think to look at their phones, which were blowing up with notifications. People were trying to be there for them, but it wasn't enough.

The "story" was everywhere... including the morning news. Genni's face was all over social media and television screens right under the word "MISSING" in big, bright letters. But this "story" wasn't the full story. None of the details were out. Nobody knew about the blood. Nobody knew about the terror she felt. Nobody saw Kathrine's trauma of knowing *something* happened but not knowing *what* happened. It's like watching a car crash about to happen, but looking away before the cars hit. You didn't hear the sounds of broken glass and crushing metal. But, know it must have happened, right? That horrible thing happened... but you didn't see it. No proof. Just a feeling.

"Am I a crazy person?" Kathrine whispered looking into her bathroom mirror. "Why am I so mad? Why did I run from her? ... Why did I run?"

Kathrine knew she was alive because she ran. She didn't stick around and wait to die the way people do in scary movies, but she wished she had stayed. She wanted to know the truth about what happened to Genni. Was she alive somewhere out there? Did she run, too? Kathrine just knew it wasn't good. And she wasn't ready for the interrogation... she was the last person to see Genni. She also wasn't ready for the questions and looks she would get every day in town. Everyone is going to want to be her friend... not for her, but for what she knew.

Natalie and Derrick were eating breakfast on the square. They were used to the smell of grease and the sizzling and popping of the food on the grill because they had breakfast there almost every morning.

"I can't believe Genni is missing," Natalie said.

"I'm sure they'll find her," Derrick said as he clinked his fork onto his plate.

Natalie looked at him as he stared down at his food. She wasn't smiling...

"I can't make it to your family dinner," he told her, finally looking up.

"Why?" she asked, cold-faced.

"I'm gonna be busy I think."

"Okay," she said. She wanted to know more, but she wasn't going to dig for information. He was her boyfriend, and she wanted him to put in an effort. But he wasn't going to open up right now, and she wasn't going to cave in. "Well, I need to head out of here," she said as she stood up from the wooden table.

Zach and Evelyn sat in their living room after cleaning the entire house. They were about to throw a Christmas party for the friend group tonight, and they wanted the first gathering at the new house to be a perfect one.

"Who all is coming?" Evelyn asked.

Zach stood up from the fluffy couch and turned the fake fireplace on. "Jasper, Natalie, Derrick."

"What about Kathrine? She has really gone through a lot and could use a good group of friends."

"Yeah, I'm good with that," Zach told her.

"This will be a good night, baby," Kathrine's mom told her. She took one hand off the steering wheel and reached over to grab Kathrine's hand. She was secretly worried about tonight, but she knew her daughter needed it.

"I know. Thank you for letting me go." She turned away from the window. "I'm going to be safe, Mom. I know how to handle myself, so I don't want you to worry."

Her mom nodded, "I'm going to worry. But, I love you."

"I love you, too."

Kathrine walked up the brick steps to knock on the front door. Evelyn jumped from the couch, smiling. She opened the door, letting the light shape to Kathrine's face. The smell of the mint candles and the sound of laughter seeped from the inside.

"Come in!" Evelyn chirped.

Kathrine walked onto the carpet and looked up. The first person she made eye contact with was Derrick. He was holding Natalie's hand, but all of his attention was on Kathrine.

5

Derrick's eyes shot open. Deer in the headlights. He thought Kathrine didn't know anything about Natalie, and he was scared it was about to get ugly. The truth is: Kathrine knew he had cheated. Kathrine wasn't going to freak out. Was she expecting to see Derrick tonight? No. But she knew how to keep her cool.

"This is Kathrine, guys! She's a great girl," Evelyn told everyone even though she didn't really know her.

Derrick was squirming in the loveseat. Natalie was starting to notice his hands were getting sweaty.

"Hey, Kathrine! I'm Jasper!" he jumped up and leaned in to hug her. He usually didn't hug like that, but he had heard that Kathrine was with Genni before she went missing... Well, everyone had heard that.

"This is Derrick and Natalie. They're dating... obviously," Evelyn laughed.

Kathrine rose her eyebrows, "Derrick, you look familiar... do I know you from somewhere?"

Natalie turned to look at Derrick for his response. He may have the looks, but he couldn't think on his feet. He never planned for this. He didn't think his girlfriend and his side-chick would run into each other like this. Especially with him in the room. Natalie let go of his sweaty hands and rubbed hers on the soft fabric of the loveseat.

Jasper was the only person in the room catching on. He never liked Derrick, after all, Natalie was his best friend and Derrick would always get in the middle of it. He grabbed his drink from the end table and spun his straw around in the ice as he waited on Derrick to respond.

"No, I don't think so," he finally responded. His face was starting to blush.

"Um. Weird," Kathrine said as she spun around and sat next to Zach.

Zach was scratching his beard trying to think of a way to kill the tension. "So... you guys wanna watch a movie? Play a game?"

"Yas, let's play a game!" Natalie said as she got up from beside Derrick.

"Okay, I'll go get the games," Zach said, jumping up from his seat.

"I'll help," Derrick said as he hustled off the couch. Zach looked back, knowing Derrick needed to talk to him about something. They turned the corner into the side game room, just out of view of the living room. Derrick grabbed Zach's shoulder.

"Dude!" Derrick squirmed.

"What is going on in there? Do you know her?" Zach pushed Derrick's hand off his shoulder.

"What is *she* doing here?"

"Kathrine is nice! She probably needs some friends right now. She's new here and one of her friends is missing and she—"

"*Who cares*?!"

Zach stepped back from Derrick. "Derrick, man, I love you... but what is your problem?"

"Nothing."

Zach waited a few seconds. He knew he would spill momentarily.

"I cheated on Natalie... with her."

"You did *what?*!"

"We just made out, and I took her out on a date. I thought she would give it up, but she didn't."

Zach turned around to grab a board game. "You've got to be kidding me..."

"No, I'm not. And Kathrine didn't know about Natalie, but I guess now she does."

"I'm not fixing this for you. Just get in there and have fun."

"Zach, what's wrong with you? We've been like brothers forever and now you're just gonna let this happen?"

"Yeah, we're brothers, but this isn't cool, and I'm not gonna let this stress me out. Can we just have a good time?" Zach walked back out into the living room. He brushed shoulders with Derrick—not on purpose—but it was warranted.

"Where'd Derrick go?" Natalie laughed.

"Uh, bathroom I think," Zach said as he put "The Game of Life" on the wooden coffee table.

6

The next day, Kathrine was sitting at Stone Bridge Park waiting to meet up with Jasper. He was wanting to take a few photos for his collection he is working on, and Kathrine was wanting a new profile picture for Instagram. A win-win. She was using a large rock as a bench that could really fit about three different people. The sun was shining above her, with the breeze making the fountain sprinkle water in her direction.

Most of the time, when there is someone looking over your shoulder… you know it. You can tell that someone is just around the corner with their focus on you. Sometimes we feel like someone is watching when there is no one near. It's strange… to feel like you're not alone. We let the mystery drive us crazy. But this time, Kathrine had no idea that there was someone behind her. Not directly behind her… but under the bridge in the distance. A red hoodie was hiding their face and identity. Even if Kathrine turned around, she may not see them. They were watching her… waiting and hoping she would walk toward the bridge. Kathrine stood up from her

35

rock and dusted herself off. A smirk emerged from the shadow of the red hoodie.

Fayetteville was still new to Kathrine, and she hadn't been to Stone Bridge Park yet. She looked around and noticed the bridge the cars would drive over. The sound of cars rippling over the concrete bounced from the pavement to the water below. She looked around the park, she was the only one there... or so she thought. She stepped closer to the bridge, peeking around at the graffiti on the side. She stepped closer, letting her toes hit the shadow cast by the bridge.

On the other side of the concrete column supporting the bridge where it meets the hill, there they were. Just waiting for her to walk under the bridge into the dark area.

Kathrine's phone started to vibrate in her pocket. "Hello?" she answered as she turned around, letting her back face the bridge. She stood still. Then, from the shadows in the corner, the person in the red hoodie stepped out. Step by step, they moved closer and closer without making a sound.

She stepped away and back toward the parking lot to meet Jasper. As she passed the rock she was sitting on earlier, she looked back to the bridge. No one.

"Cool place," she whispered to herself.

"Why'd you have to be like that?!" Derrick yelled at Kathrine. He lunged forward and turned the radio volume all the way down.

After her photo shoot with Jasper, she met up with Derrick in the new fried-chicken fast food restaurant's parking lot.

"You were cheating on Natalie with me. You have *issues*, you know that?"

"Shut your mouth," he pointed at her. "She isn't perfect, and I wanted a night with a little more."

"You're disgusting. And you know what, you shouldn't be mad at me. I knew before last night. I'm not dumb... and people talk."

"Who?" he asked, tightening his grip on the steering wheel.

Kathrine knew what she was doing. Genni told her that night, but she wanted to mess up Derrick. She wanted his brain to spiral as if it wasn't already.

"Who!?" he screamed.

"Don't you dare raise your voice at me," she said as she swung the car door open. Kathrine jumped out of his vehicle. "You'll get what's coming to you. Don't play games, Derrick." She slammed his door.

"Zach," he whispered to himself. He hit his steering wheel thinking it would make him feel better.

"He knew. He invited that rat on purpose." Derrick slammed his keys into the ignition. He pulled out of the parking lot and was headed straight for Zach's house.

7

He couldn't stop thinking about it. Derrick was letting his anger get the best of him. He started swerving between cars and through the one strip in town. The light at the high school turned red, but he hit the gas. To the right, a blue car was pulling out of the new fast food restaurant. Derrick didn't care... his anger was boiling to new levels. The driver of the blue car hit the horn as Derrick sped by. They swerved back onto the side of the road to avoid him. The smell of burnt rubber seeped from the road as Derrick slammed on his breaks and skid into the next lane. He looked back, shocked that he let that happen... but once he realized nobody was hurt, he turned back to the gas pedal and steering wheel.

He slid into Zach's driveway shooting gravel out from below his tires. Zach jumped up from the couch and ran to the window.

What the heck? he thought.

Derrick slammed on his breaks and stomped to the front door. His arms were swinging by his sides. He slammed his hands on the door as hard as he could.

Bang! Bang! Bang!

"Zach! Hey!" Derrick growled.

Zach slid from the window to the front door.

"What is it?" he asked after opening the loud, squeaking door.

Derrick leaned into Zach, making him move backward into the house. Derrick's bushy eyebrows were tilted in, intimidating Zach. This was a new feeling for him... he had never been in a serious confrontation. He bumped into the loveseat and leaned back onto the arm of the chair. He looked like a pitiful, cornered animal.

Derrick and Zach had the same thing happening on the inside. Adrenaline was pumping through their veins. Their heart was pounding in their throats. Time was almost in slow motion with a red filter. One was anger. One was panic.

"You really have some balls, don't you?" Derrick snarled.

"What is wrong with you, Derrick!? You really need to chill," Zach tried to resolve the situation even though his hands were shaking.

"I need to chill!?" Derrick rose his index finger to Zach's face. "You're the only one that needs to chill here. You run that mouth..."

"What are you talking about?" Zach's eyes were wide.

"Stay away from me. Stay away from Natalie. Stay away from Kathrine... actually, no. *You* can have Kathrine. That's probably why you did it anyways."

"Did what, Derrick?" Zach finally had a sternness to his voice.

Derrick pushed Zach in his chest, knocking him back into the loveseat. "You don't know when to stop, do you?"

"Get out of my house," Zach said, trying to keep his cool.

Evelyn emerged from the hallway. "Boys, what in God's name is going on in here?"

"Get out!" Zach yelled.

Derrick gave Zach the middle finger and walked to the door. He wanted to leave the door open to show he didn't care about them, but his anger wanted him to do something else. He slammed the door so hard the new family picture fell off the wall. The glass didn't shatter but the frame was broken.

"What is going on, Zach?" Evelyn asked at the verge of tears.

"Derrick has lost it. He thinks I ratted him out."

"Ratted him out? About what?"

"Kathrine. Natalie." Zach grabbed his phone and typed in Kathrine's name. "He cheated on Natalie and had Kathrine fooled, too. He thinks I told Kathrine that she was the side-chick."

"What are you doing?" she asked. He didn't answer. "Zach, I don't think you should call the police..."

"I'm not. I'm calling Kathrine."

"What's she going to do?"

"She knows more than I do..."

"Well... be careful out there. I don't know how safe it is anymore..."

42

8

"Are you serious? He really did that?" Kathrine asked Zach. She was putting her blonde hair into a messy bun like she was ready to fight. She wasn't going to, but it made her feel more prepared. Any time Derrick is brought up she gets heated. Sometimes her fists even ball up.

"Yes, I'm for real. Kat, he scared me. He really did," Zach was being honest with her. He didn't care if he looked like a wimp. It was an actual confrontation, and he didn't really know what to do.

"What do we do?" she asked.

"Police. We call the police and let them know how aggressive he is. Listen to this... you move here from Florida. Derrick cheats on Natalie with you. Genni gets too close and his anger gets the best of him. He kills Genni and hides her body... Kat, he was probably stalking you that night." Kathrine looked to the floor. "And then, he thinks everything is fixed and he could leave you alone. But Evelyn invites you over that night and everything explodes. His plan went up in flames and now he is pissed and trying to find a way out. He is a loose cannon. I'm ready to tell the cops." Zach leaned against the granite counter in Kathrine's new kitchen.

"I don't know, Zach. I get it, but it doesn't all add up. It's a little too drastic." Kathrine was trying to tone down Zach's excitement. She was getting really good at hiding her mess of emotions. Practice makes perfect, right? But on the inside, she wasn't okay. Like a rat hiding in a dark corner, she tried to push back everything... but when the flashbacks hit, she can't.

"What do you mean?"

"Derrick confronting you... I mean... I think it's just drama. He didn't hurt you or anything. There isn't really evidence of him threatening you. Trust me, I've seen my fair share of trouble back in Florida..."

Zach rolled his eyes and started rubbing his beard. "We have to do something."

"Where is he?"

"Probably at Natalie's... or home."

"Let's go riding. We're going to find his car and search it."

"What? Are you kidding me?!" Zach said, but he grabbed his keys. Yes, he was scared, and his heart rate was starting to pick up... but it was time to do something about Derrick.

Nothing was distracting him from looking for that car. Kathrine was perched up on the leather seat looking out the open window. The wind was knocking her hair back as they rolled through the backroads looking for Derrick's house.

But then, his eyes couldn't stay on the road... Kathrine was just too beautiful. He looked a little longer. Then a little longer. He would keep staring, but Derrick's house was up ahead.

"There it is," she said.

Zach pulled off to the side of the road and turned off his headlights.

"It's probably locked." Zach turned off his car.

Kathrine slowly pushed the door open and stepped out onto the pothole-scattered backroad. The night was a dark one. The moon was full, and the stars were scattered. There wasn't any clouds or noises to take away from the beauty in the nature above them, but they didn't notice. They leaned down and made their way to Derrick's car.

Then it hit: panic. The idea that whoever did that to Genni could do it again.

Her eyes started looking at Zach instead of Derrick's car. She slowed down, and so did he, which for some reason made her panic more. She jumped up to her feet, making sure she could run if she had to.

"No," she said as she stepped away from Zach. "Don't do this." That's all her fear would let her whisper.

9

"What are you talking about?" Zach responded in a snippy voice.

"Get away from me," Kathrine's voice was changing from a whisper to almost a scream. Her bottom lip was starting to quiver. Trauma and nerves come together, and she couldn't get the image of that night out of her head.

"Just trust me. Look," Zach said as he reached into his pockets and emptied them. He opened his hands to show her... empty. Nothing. "I don't want to hurt you. I *can't* hurt you. We're here to look for Derrick's stuff. We need to get in his car. Why would I do this?"

Kathrine froze... not knowing what Zach's intentions were. She thought of how things were back in Florida. She thought she had gotten away from the sudden anxiety attacks... but it looked like they were back.

"Breathe. In and out. In and out," he told her.

She looked around... nothing. He didn't have anything to hurt her with, and she had to trust someone, even if she didn't believe it.

"I'm sorry."

"I'm sorry, too. It's okay," Zach apologized. He wasn't quite sure what he did to cause this, but he still wanted to say sorry.

"Do you still want to dig around in his car?" Kathrine asked.

He looked over to Derrick's car. "If you still want to..." he said, hoping she still wanted to, too.

"Yeah... sure." She nodded.

They crouched as they got closer to Derrick's house. There was only one light on inside... the TV. The different colors of light and constant change were unpredictable, but it wasn't anywhere near bright enough to see Kathrine and Zach.

They crept to the door.

Please, you're pretty dumb, Derrick ... don't tell me you locked your car, Kathrine thought. She coiled her fingers around the cold door handle.

48

Click.

The metal separated and revealed the interior. The light turned on, and Kathrine slammed her hand on the roof, searching for the switch to turn it off. Zach was on the other side of the car, looking through the passenger side window. His side was locked.

"Here." Kathrine hit the unlock button after turning the lights off.

"Wait, I'm not sure what I'm looking for..." Zach said.

"A crowbar," she swallowed her fear. "It was a crowbar."

Kathrine started digging in the console between the seats while Zach dug into the glove department.

"Ew," she said.

"What is it?"

"Snot rags. Ugh," she shook her hand away.

Zach started laughing, then looked up at the house. *Too loud*, he thought.

Kathrine turned and started looking in the backseat. "I hate this car." Her memory flashed of that night after the movies.

She started feeling around in the seats, then to the floorboard. Her fingers ran over the carpet. A bottle. A bag. Then, something metal... she grabbed the cold object and pulled it closer to the window, using the moonlight to see.

"Oh, my God."

A crowbar. But, not just any crowbar. A crowbar covered in dry blood.

10

Sheriff Mullins' desk was getting full of papers and pictures. He needed this mystery to all come together, and fast. Fayetteville has had murders before, but this one was horribly different. It was a teenaged girl. The thing was, she was technically just missing. Social media and "the talk of the town" was that Genni was dead. The 17-year-old girl, Beta Club member, energized part of the community, was gone. Yes, the scene looked like a murder... but there wasn't a body. And the girl that reported it, Kathrine, didn't see it happen... she just had a feeling.

There was bleach in her blood according to the samples taken from the scene. Oh, the blood. There was so much... she could have bled out... *if it were all hers.* There was also deer's blood in the mix. Honestly, it looked like someone had dumped deer blood all around the crime scene to make it look like Genni bled more than she did. Genni's blood was there, but it wasn't all hers.

Kathrine told him that the killer (or kidnapper) had a crowbar and was wearing a red hoodie with the strings tightly closing the opening to hide their face. That's all? That's all she could remember? There were way too many holes in this story.

Speaking of holes, there was one that was getting deeper and deeper. Genni's parents have been at his desk all the time. They had taken off from work to grieve—which is only fair—and been driving, searching, calling... doing whatever they can. Sheriff Mullins prayed he would see Genni. Find her and take her straight to her parents. He couldn't stand to see parents hurt in this way...

So this is what he had:

Genni's blood.

Deer blood.

Bleach.

Two terrified parents.

One terrified town...

But what he didn't have: a body or an answer.

He pulled out Kathrine's police report and ran his finger over the wrinkled paper. He stopped at her phone number and started to dial. *No*, he thought. He set the phone back where it belonged on his desk. *I need to go home. It's so late already*, he thought.

But today was his lucky day. He didn't need to call Kathrine. She was pulling into the parking lot with Zach, bringing the weapon of concern: the crowbar... *Derrick's* crowbar.

11

"I love this place," Jasper said as he bit into his 6-inch sub.

"It's okay," Evelyn chuckled as she sipped on her lemonade. Her side of the table was empty. She never really liked Subway. She thought all the choices were too much to handle. The sauces. The bread. The peppers… She liked things more organized and concrete. Sure, it was just a sandwich, but she'd rather have a burger.

"Derrick is in some trouble with Natalie… that night was crazy. Like, you could feel the tension," Jasper rubbed away a small piece of lettuce from his mouth.

"What was he thinking? And he had the nerve to come to our house and scream at Zach."

"Hold on," Jasper put down the sub as if it made a difference. "When did this happen?" He leaned in.

"Just the other day. I had to walk in there to make them shut up. It was something about Zach telling Kathrine about him cheating."

"Oh, yeah, I guess she didn't know at the time?"

"Definitely not. But she knew when she walked through the door."

Jasper then changed the subject to something a little deeper. He was always playful, but he was always thinking, too. "You know, it's so sad how they treated Kathrine."

"How who treated her?" Evelyn asked. She took another sip of her lemonade.

"People in this town. They stare and look at her. She said that some people even question her. This is a serious thing! Like, Genni is missing, and some people kinda act like it's a game."

"I wish it was that simple... you're right. It's really sad," Evelyn paused and looked deep into Jasper's eyes. She knew his past. How people used to treat him. Jasper knew how hard things could be. In fact, Evelyn was one of the few people that was nice to him in middle school.

"Yeah, it can be tough sometimes." Jasper looked back down at his sandwich.

Jasper was always so close to his mom. He loved her like his friend. Was it weird? No. That's his mom, and they love each other unconditionally. You'd think a parent/child relationship that strong wouldn't cause any hurt, any pain... but it did.

They spent so much time together while Jasper's dad was always on the road that he picked up her habits. He liked the shows she did. He liked the music she did. She influenced him in all the right ways. But to others, it wasn't *just* an influence.

Jasper liked a certain type of music. He liked certain shows. He talked with his hands. He talked a certain way. He didn't drink alcohol. He didn't chew tobacco. He didn't smoke. He didn't party every weekend and hook up with as many girls as he could. In the eyes of his high school, that made him gay. He grew up with that label: gay.

Because if Jasper liked girls, it didn't matter... it was a lie to his peers that walked the halls at school.

"Do you even have one?"

"Why does your voice sound like that? Don't answer that... we already know."

"I see you looked at me, faggot. Don't even think about trying to be my friend. Don't talk to me."

The laughing. The pointing. The texts. The looks.

Jasper wasn't like the typical person. He was straight, but it didn't matter. He was *different*, so he was wrong.

But after all of this, he always made the best he could in life. And here he was in Subway eating with a good friend. He didn't get near as many looks anymore. Maybe he "grew out of it." Really, it doesn't matter anymore, because Jasper finally was treated the way he should: like everyone else.

But maybe Jasper wasn't like everyone else... because not everyone was on that scribbled, hidden piece of paper. Jasper was on a list. A kill list.

12

Evelyn finished her lemonade. The conversation with Jasper was beyond small talk. It was going deeper, to the meaty topics she loved to talk about, and so did he.

"How is it living with Zach? I know this is still fresh to you guys," Jasper said.

"Yeah. It's still fresh. To be honest, I'm mad. Our parents just ditch our families and get together. Now I'm step-siblings with someone I was just acquainted with. Then, our parents take off on some honeymoon. What were they thinking?"

"Do they even know about what's been happening here? About Genni?"

"If they had social media, but they're in some cabin or something... I don't know. We can't contact them. They said we probably wouldn't be able to talk to them. I don't know if I want to, if I'm being honest."

"That's weird." Jasper didn't think about overstepping a boundary by calling her parent and step-parent weird. Good thing she didn't notice... or care.

Evelyn shrugged her shoulders and rolled her eyes. She danced the ice around in her cup.

"If it makes you feel any better, my parents fight all the time," he told her.

"Ah, the luxury of having parents that aren't divorced."

"It's rare... but my parents act like it anyways. Sometimes they don't even notice me. It's like I'm not even there."

That hit Evelyn. She hated everything about it. "I'm sorry, Jasper."

"No! It's okay. I'm not in a fit over it. It is what it is. I'm about to graduate and Lord knows where I'm going next."

Jasper had his camera and the town square. He loved the blinking traffic lights this late at night. The yellow put a new tint on the pavement that he felt was unique. The road was empty, so it was a perfect place to practice his new photography tricks. No one was out at this time of night... so he thought. His denim jacket wasn't keeping in enough warmth, but he didn't care. He liked the lighting, and he loved this surge of inspiration he was feeling. He leaned down and put one knee on the ground. He leaned to the left, hitting the button. *Click*. The shutter in the camera flashed open to take the picture.

Yes, it was a beautiful scene. His camera was capturing something that would look great on Instagram. But, something a little more exciting was behind him. At the street corner by the Coca-Cola mural on the brick wall... someone was watching. But, he'd never see who they were... the red hoodie was hiding their face.

13

Jasper stood up, letting his camera fall back down into his chest. He looked down at the screen of his camera as he scrolled through his new yellow pictures. Standing in the middle of the road with the yellow blinking light flashing above his head, he suddenly was somewhere else. He went too far in his gallery and the memories started rolling like a supercut. It was pictures of his best friend, Natalie. At this point, everyone but Natalie knows about Derrick cheating on her. Jasper's secret was that he loved Natalie... He loved the way they laughed together. The way they were like puzzle pieces. She loved puzzles... Jasper hated them, but he would solve them with her. Natalie was the girl out of his reach. She was with the "bad boy," and he didn't think that would change.

He also didn't see the person in the red hoodie behind him. But then, he heard a car coming from the left. Up the hill, the lights pushed up the incline to show the wall of the building on the corner. The Coca-Cola mural glowed in the headlights.

The person in the red hoodie freaked out. They pulled the strings of the hoodie tight to hide their face even more.

The light was trying to seep through the hoodie and onto their face. Jasper turned around to see them hurrying away.

Strange, he thought. He brought his camera up to his face as fast as he could.

Snap. A photo.

The left of the image was framed by the red brick and the Coca-Cola mural. The lights from the car made the subject of the photo shine: the person in the red hoodie. It was like a rare, mythical creature captured on film. Like the Patterson-Gimlin film of Bigfoot or the photo of the Lochness Monster. But, Jasper didn't know what he had just taken, or the danger he was in.

He looked down at the photo. *Not good enough. Exposure's off*, he thought. He was always so critical of himself, and he put his finger on the delete button.

"Hey, kid! What are you doing?"

Jasper looked up at the car, still in the middle of the road.

"Can you move, please?!" the guy in the car yelled out the window.

"Oh! Sorry!" Jasper zoned back into reality. He stepped to the side of the road, letting the car pass. He turned the camera off and walked to his car, leaving his "bad" photo still in the gallery.

He may not have liked his photo, but it made him think. It popped a question into his head: *who was that?*

14

Natalie walked from the dark kitchen to meet Derrick in the living room. He was shaking his head at the floor like he had reached his end. His fidgeting was getting faster: the tapping of his foot, the pulling of the thread in the couch cushion, the rubbing on his neck.

The only sounds in the house were the pops of the wood in the walls as they settled. Derrick's dad was almost never home, so Natalie and Derrick were home alone.

"When are you going to open up and talk to me? All I see is you in a twist and blowing up all over the place. And over what? Apparently everyone knows but me, and that's messed up."

"You don't have to know everything, Natalie."

"What are you talking about?! We're dating! Something tells me you're supposed to talk to me about stuff... I'm not your ragdoll. I'm not some lost puppy that follows you around. And let me tell you something," Natalie leaned in closer to Derrick. She held her hand right in front of his face, hovering her index finger just above her thumb. "I'm this close to leaving you. You don't know what it means to be a man. You don't know how to love somebody."

"You're helping so much!" Derrick's sarcasm was a mix between spite and bitterness. "You want to know everything. Why can't you sit there and look pretty? 'Bout all you're good at anyways."

That was it... "Get out, Derrick!" Her yell made him jump. He'd never gotten this much aggression out of her, even when he deserved it.

"This is *my* house. What are you talking about? *You* get out," he pointed at her.

"I wasn't talking about this house. Get out of my *life*."

It finally hit him. He dropped his head and let his anger turn into hurt for the first time in a long time. Natalie leaned against the wall and let him take it in. Now, she felt like he was listening for the first time.

"Derrick, you have to see where I'm coming from."

"You don't think I feel bad?" His voice was much lower; his soft side was coming out. "How do you think I feel,

Natalie? Zach was my best friend, and he thinks he can go and snitch on me," he uttered.

They both paused. Derrick knew he said too much. Natalie smirked because that's all she could do.

"What did he snitch on, Derrick?"

"Nothing, Natalie. It's whatever." The silence between them couldn't describe the horrible tension in the room. It was like a rope being pulled at both ends, and Natalie was almost ready to let go.

Natalie's phone rattled on the coffee table.

Natalie, this is serious. Derrick is up to a lot of stuff right now. Gosh I'm really worried about you... Can I call? Zach texted her.

It buzzed loudly in the silence. She saw the name plastered across the pixels on her screen. Her eyes shot open, knowing that if Derrick saw it, the room would explode. She grabbed her phone, read the message, and went to his front porch.

"Hey, what's up?" she said, putting the cold phone to her cheek.

"Where are you?" Zach asked.

"Derrick's house, why?"

"You have to get out, now."

"What are you talking about? I can handle him. I won't let him hurt me."

Natalie didn't notice it, but Derrick stood up from the couch and turned the corner to the front door. He crept closer and closer, avoiding the spots on the floor that make the loud pops. His figure moved slowly in the darkness, getting closer... and closer...

"Do you really think he'd hurt me?" she asked.

15

"It's not Derrick. It can't be Derrick."

"Natalie, you've been pushed away and hidden for so long. Please, listen to me and get out of there." Zach was desperate, and she could hear it in his voice.

Derrick's presence was hovering in the open door frame. He managed to creep the door open without her noticing. It wasn't like most front doors; it was quiet. And he used that to his advantage. He stepped out onto the cold, wooden front porch.

"Okay. I'm sorry, Zach. I'm leaving his house now." Natalie told him on the phone, not knowing Derrick was standing right behind her. If only she knew... she would never have to live with what happened next. The wrong place, the wrong time. It was one word. One name.

He *snapped*.

Derrick lunged forward, knocking Natalie off the porch and onto the shivering blades of grass and mud puddles.

Natalie's hair flung around her face, some of the frosty red mud splashing on her now rosy cheeks. She landed on her hands, letting her phone rumble to the grass. Zach was still on the phone listening to the struggle.

Derrick bucked his shoulders up, trying to show his dominance over her. He hopped off the porch and landed on his feet in front of her. He pushed her foot out of his way with a kick.

"You did that to Genni," she tried to gasp out. Her lungs were struggling for air from the impact of the ground. Her breath was long gone.

"I didn't touch Genni."

"Shocking," she tried to snap as much as she could. The fighter in her was loading up and ready to launch. She bundled the grass in her fist, and when her breath was finally back… she didn't let go of the tension in her hands. She ripped the grass up, roots and all, to try to punch him. She was on the ground, but close enough to go for his knees.

Derrick was too big. Too strong.

He grabbed her grass-filled fists and slung her down on her back. He leaned down over her.

"Help! He's going to kill me! Just like he did Genni!" she yelled, praying Zach was listening. The phone had dimmed, but the two bars of signal was enough for Zach to hear it.

Derrick grabbed both of her cheeks with one hand, covering her mouth from any cry for help.

Derrick's anger was like a pot forgotten on a glowing red stove. It was boiling to a new temperature every minute. Sometimes, he was able to turn the temperature down, but not now... definitely not right now. His anger was bubbling over the brim of the pot. Blinding. Red. Sizzling. Powerful.

He couldn't see anymore. His brain was spinning into darkness, with his strength pressuring his "girlfriend" into the ground. At this point, she was so helpless. Any move she made he would counter it. There was nothing she could do, but she was trying everything.

Natalie was the noodle stuck in the boiling pot. No way out. Not anymore. The pot was boiling over, and you couldn't even see her anymore.

In the distance, a buzz. A hum. A spinning siren.

Blue lights danced in circles with red ones. Bouncing off the naked trees and pavement. The lights were coming down and coming fast, waking everyone on this back road in Fayetteville.

She was crying and yelling at Derrick. But, Sheriff Mullins was louder.

"Cool it, kid! Step away and put your hands up. Now!"

16

Derrick's foot was bouncing on the concrete floor. The silver table was cold and let the bright light above it bounce into his eyes. The mirror on the wall in front of him was massive, covering almost the entire wall. His chair was uncomfortable and made his butt hurt. He looked at the heavy metal door, waiting for someone to walk in and sit in front of him.

He ran his hands through his hair the best he could with them latched together by handcuffs. He let them drop onto the table. *Clink.* The handcuffs were heavy, and so was the situation he was in.

How did this happen... how did it get so bad... he thought.

The heavy door squealed on the floor like nails on a chalkboard. Sheriff Mullins knew it made that sound, and he did it on purpose. He stepped into the room just enough for the door to slam behind him. He stared at Derrick with disappointment. He had so much he wanted to say to the boy that didn't know how to be a man. But as sheriff, he couldn't let his personal feelings get in the way. He never did, but with a murder case cutting deep into the stress of the entire police force and the town, Derrick just might get what he deserves.

Derrick opened his hands and slightly shook his head at the sheriff; he was trying to prompt him into breaking the silence. Sheriff Mullins moved over to the table and sat down, letting the leather in his boots squeak on the floor. Their eyes met as much as they could. Sheriff Mullins was tall and buff, and Derrick's teenaged-muscle was nothing in comparison.

"Was it something she said?" he asked. His deep voice carried between the concrete walls.

"What are you talking about?" Derrick mumbled.

"Why were you on top of her in the yard?"

"I don't know. She was disrespecting me."

"And that's enough to do *what* to her? What were your intentions, son?"

"My intentions?"

"What was your goal… What were you trying to do?"

"Let me guess, you think I was going to try to kill her. Are you kidding me?" Derrick dropped his hands into his lap.

73

He let the silence linger in the room for a moment. "We've got a missing girl that's probably dead. And you're fighting your girlfriend in your yard…" Sheriff Mullins looked back at the mirror to signal the people behind the glass. "Genni is missing and everyone is upset. But listen, son, I think she might not be with us anymore. The scene looked pretty violent… did you know she was hit with a crowbar?"

"A crowbar?" Derrick didn't look up. He kept shaking his head. "No."

Sheriff Mullins rose his hand to signal a deputy. She walked in holding a crowbar in a plastic bag. She dropped the weapon onto the table. It was heavy, and the drop was louder than Derrick was expecting; it made him jump. He started rubbing his neck with his restrained hands.

"I've never seen this," Derrick said.

"Why did we find it in your car?"

Derrick's eyes shot open, finally looking back up at the sheriff. "What!? This is not mine!" his voice was beginning to shake.

"The stuff on this crowbar has three things in it… bleach, deer's blood, and Genni's blood. Son, all of those things were at the crime scene. Do you hear what I'm saying?" He leaned in over the table towards Derrick. "This crowbar was at the crime scene and probably was used to kill Genni... and we found it in your car."

Derrick dropped his head. "I want a lawyer and my phone call."

"I figured so," Sheriff Mullins stood up, pushed his chair back to the table and left the interrogation room. The woman that brought in the crowbar was still behind the glass watching him. Sheriff Mullins stood next to her looking at Derrick.

"Did he do it?" she asked him.

"I don't know yet..." he paused. "I want to talk to the kids that brought us the crowbar first."

17

"I don't like this, man," the teenager told his dad as they went to the edge of the freezing cold water.

"It's okay, son. I told you this is the tradition. All the men in this family do this at some point. It's the way we do things."

The Thompsons did this with every father and son at the edge of the Elk River. It was used as some type of bonding time within the family. They thought it met the quota of "bonding time" for the fathers and sons of every generation in the family.

The breeze was soft and so was the flow of the river. It was low and barely moving, the winter weather made it too cold to handle, but for this family, it was something you had to do.

The son took off his shoes and set them onto the dirty rocks at the water's edge. He let the water tickle his toes, sending goosebumps up his feet to his ankles.

"There you go. I'm right behind you," the dad told him.

He stepped forward into the water towards the rocky, dirty sandbar where a pillar from the old bridge stood. The stone had dead vines climbing it to the very top. The water was low, and he was able to get to the island easily. He shook his hands in hopes the water wouldn't freeze his insides.

At the rocky island, the dad placed his hand on his son's shoulder. "I knew you could do it, son."

"Thanks, Dad," he said, even though he thought it was stupid. He knew he wouldn't do this with his son.

The son reached down and grabbed a rock, throwing it into the water in front of him.

Clonk. The rock bounced back up and fell into the water to the right. Then, a shoe rippled its way to the rock island. A solid-red shoe with white laces. The dirt from the bottom of the river had stained the rim around the sole of the shoe. The son picked it up and handed it to his dad.

"This is weird."

"Nah, I'm sure someone lost it recently," he stopped. For a moment, he agreed. Who would be out here and lose a shoe in this cold water? No one would be out here, except them. Then came the urge to show his masculinity and leadership to his son, he leaped into the water without warning. He left the shoe behind as he trudged his way to through the water.

"What are you doing?" his son asked from the tiny island.

"Ah, come on! It's not that bad!" he yelled back.

Then, his foot hit something strange, and he stopped in the water. Letting the ripples around him slow to a stop. He reached below the surface of the water and grabbed a rope. His fist pulled at the shirt on the other side. It was heavy. The rope. The cinder blocks. The water weight. The *dead* weight.

He struggled to pull it up out of the water. He tugged with both hands, almost losing his balance in the water.

Finally, he pulled up a dead girl's body. Her neck showed a gruesome scene. The massive gash from the crowbar was ugly. Her head flopped back, letting her wet hair fall behind her. It revealed her muddy, eroded face. It wasn't hard to tell.

This was Genni.

18

Sheriff Mullins' head was rested in his hands. The files and information decorated the top of the desk in a messy fashion. Papers here. Papers there. The phone was beginning to feel warm because he was using it all the time.

"Listen, it's wrong that he did that to his girl, and if she wants to press charges, then that boy will be in a mess. He has a temper that I don't think he can control, obviously."

"His parents are going to cause a problem. They've always had trouble between them. His dad breathes drama, so does his mom. We've got to handle this right. They're going to blow it up, and there will be news stations on us. Everything like that," she sat down on the leather chair in front of his desk.

"It's all falling into place don't you think? We've got the suspect. We've got the weapon. He looks so suspicious."

His deputy pulled her hair behind her ears, "I know what you're thinking."

"It's too perfect. I don't think it was him," he started to point at the different files on his desk. "The body is hidden perfectly. Deer's blood and bleach at the scene. Everything is taken care of to hide any lead. Then, he's stupid enough to leave the murder weapon in his back seat? With blood and everything else from the scene?" he paused... "I don't think Derrick did it."

Natalie looked into her bathroom mirror of her hospital room, crying as she examined the bruises Derrick gave her. Her feelings for Derrick were no longer pretty. The truth is, she was never in love. She knew he was a cheater, and she finally got what she needed.

Jasper was scrolling through the pictures in his camera. When he got to Natalie's pictures, he stopped scrolling. He was letting his crush conquer his mind. He couldn't stop thinking about her, just like every other night. The girl he loved was with the bad boy.

Zach's buddy, Derrick, had gone too far. He cheated. He lied. He argued. Zach was stressed out from this entire situation, but he couldn't help but think about how much he had caused and what he had done...

Evelyn kept trying to distract her mind by playing silly games on her phone, but it wasn't working. She sat in her living room waiting on her mom and new step-dad to finally return from their honeymoon. Zach and Evelyn had so much to tell them, but could they tell everything?

Derrick sat in the jail holding unit waiting on his lawyer and phone call. His life was falling apart. No, he couldn't control his anger. Everything was out of hand. *I've got to go out swinging at this point*, he thought.

Kathrine hated the fact that she had to move to Fayetteville. She felt at home in Florida, and now that was stripped away. She was still new here, and everything was blowing up. She left Florida for a reason, and it looked like she brought her secrets and problems with her.

Someone killed Genni. Someone had a list. And Sheriff Mullins had his hands full.

19

"Long time no see," Sheriff Mullins said as he sat in front of Kathrine in the interrogation room. He gave her a cup of coffee to keep her awake. It was obvious she didn't need it because her feet were bouncing on the concrete floor nonstop and her fingers kept fidgeting from her hair to her neck. He just wanted to make her feel at home.

"I don't really like coffee, but thank you," Kathrine told him, pushing it back to his side of the table. The smell was strong and bitter. It was obvious there wasn't anything in it.

"Oh, that's all right. I'll drink it." He let about a third of the cup fall down his throat, not letting the temperature or bitterness affect him. "I don't really like anything in my coffee."

"That's gross," she chuckled. It didn't take her anxiousness away, but it helped.

"So, I brought you in today to talk about Derrick. You reported the murder to me, and you also found the crowbar with Zach. Let's talk about that—"

❖ ❖ ❖

In the next room, Deputy Marie Evans was talking to and questioning Zach. They thought Kathrine might have been the more nervous of the two, but Zach was really uneasy.

"I didn't do anything. I promise," he hurried his hands through his hair.

"I know, hun. We didn't call you in here like you did something. We just want some more information," she walked to the mirror in the room and waved her hand. This was something they used to make the suspect feel more comfortable, to think the people watching on the other side of the glass had walked away. They didn't, but it fooled Zach.

"What do you know about Derrick?" she asked him.

"We used to be best friends. Then, he cheated on his girlfriend, Natalie."

"What a shame," she smiled and walked back to her seat. "And he cheated on Natalie with who?"

Zach pointed at the door. "Kathrine. Who I came here with. I was with her when we found the crowbar."

"What do you know about Kathrine?"

"I know she moved here from Florida. She was trying to fit in here, I guess, and she ended up with Derrick. But, she's not like that. She didn't know about Natalie."

"Do you think Kathrine would not like Derrick for any reason?" she moved the hair from her forehead and back into the bushy, short haircut.

"...Yes. She doesn't like him, but who does?" he started twirling his thumbs.

Deputy Evans stared into Zach's eyes... not for intimidation, but as a warning. She bounced her focus from his left eye to his right, making her eyes dart back and forth. "Thank you for coming out, hun. You can leave now."

Zach nodded and stood up from his chair. He reached out over the table for a handshake. She grabbed his hand as ladylike as she could. Zach let go and headed for the door. Before he could leave the room, she turned around to talk to him one last time.

"Hey, hun," she felt like she needed to tell him something. It was bothering her, and she liked the kid. "You really don't know everyone. People are crazy these days and you never know... be careful out there."

Zach met up with Kathrine and her mom in the lobby before walking out to the parking lot together. Kathrine walked through the door, brushing her blonde hair behind her ear to stop the wind from blowing it. Zach stared at her... letting two questions run through his head.

Why did she come to Fayetteville? What happened in Florida?

20

"Thank you," Natalie told the nurse as she washed her hands. The water pressure made some splash out of the silver sink. "I know I'm going to be okay. He's scary, but I mean, I'm fine."

The nurse turned to Natalie's step-dad. "Do what you can to keep her away from that guy. I'm not a cop, but I have children of my own. Protect her." Even though Genni's body being found wasn't out to the public yet, she was on everyone's mind.

"Thank you, ma'am. She'll be fine." Natalie's step-dad was always there for her. He shook the nurse's hand and started for the door. Natalie hopped off the examining table and joined him.

Robert wrapped his coat around Natalie on their way to the truck. He let his arms covered in tattoos show; Jesus's name and crosses danced on his arms in ink. He was unashamed of his faith.

The glowing red lights on the hospital created a red spotlight over the dark parking lot. Their shadows moved with them in the night. They opened the doors and talked as he drove her home.

"He hit you?" he asked, not taking his eyes off the road.

"He *threw* me. Off the freaking porch, too. He was on top of me, and I thought I was going to die," Natalie was holding back her tears. "Are we pressing charges?"

Robert assumed Derrick was already in a holding cell at the jail. He would know... he'd been there before. "It's up to you, Nat."

"I don't want him to go to jail forever. I want a restraining order or something. But, he doesn't need to go to jail. Not yet."

Robert looked over to Natalie as he slowed at the red light. "Do you still love him?"

"No," she whispered. Letting the red light bounce off the tear on her cheek. She sniffed, then looked out the window.

"I want you to be able to defend yourself, Nat. We'll do whatever we have to. I know it's a long drive out to our place, but—"

"Where's Mom?"

"She should be on her way home now. Her phone died earlier today so we couldn't get in touch."

"I just really want to see her," Natalie put her head in her hands.

As they finally pulled into their driveway twenty minutes later, Robert opened the glove box in front of Natalie.

"You don't have a permit yet, but we can work on that. I think you need this." He grabbed something in the shadows of the glove box. He pulled it out and turned on the overhead light in the car. "Here. I trust you, and you know what's appropriate with this."

He placed a heavy, black pistol on Natalie's lap. She picked it up like a pro... because she'd used one before.

21

Evelyn threw the Sour Patch Kids bag at Jasper. The sugar rattled in the plastic bag as he caught it.

"You hate the oranges or something?" he asked.

"Eww. They're disgusting," she told him.

"Well," he popped one into his mouth. "They're my favorite."

"I know you told me your parents were being a pain the other day. How are they? Is it still a mess at home?" she leaned back into the seat as she looked at the burning fake fireplace in her living room.

"I'm ready for Christmas break to be over. I'm ready to get out of the house," he told her, dropping the candy to the end table.

"It's that bad?"

"Yeah," he whispered.

"Well, my parents are back finally. They're so obsessed with themselves... it's so annoying—"

"Evelyn," the deep voice from the kitchen made her jump. "Come here."

She looked at Jasper, wide-eyed.

"Oops," Jasper whispered.

"This will be fun..."

"I'll let you handle that. I'm gonna roll out." Jasper grabbed the Sour Patch Kids and ran for the door. He had enough issues with his parents, and he didn't want to see Evelyn get in trouble for talking about hers.

It was Christmas Eve. It was unusually warm this winter, but still too cold to forget your jacket. But the warm weather wasn't enough to make the people of Fayetteville hide their holiday spirit. Christmas music still played in cars as they drove through town. The Christmas lights were still hanging from the doors of every business.

Kathrine, Zach, Evelyn, and Jasper sat together at a table in McDonald's. The windows were covered in holiday stickers and paintings. The group hadn't been able to meet up in a while. But this time, someone was missing. They were all okay with it, too. Derrick was still dealing with whatever mess he was in now, and Natalie never wanted to see him again.

"He can stay away as far as I'm concerned," Jasper said.

"Yeah, he's honestly scary..." Evelyn said. "The way he's just this loose cannon. I don't want to be around him!"

Natalie pulled her hat lower down her forehead. "I'd rather not talk about him right now."

"I get that," Kathrine grabbed another handful of fries.

Zach didn't know what to say, so he took a sip of his free water. He grabbed his phone and opened Facebook. He scrolled past the top post to find something everyone was talking about.

The official police statement regarding the tragic death of Genesis Fisher is attached below. She was a great part of this town that we will never forget. This a joint release with Genesis' family. The Facebook post had over 450 comments. Most of them said either "Praying" or something sad. There was also the occasional harassing comment from someone like "If that were my child, I wouldn't be making a statement. The parents obviously did it for attention!" and other ridiculous comments that are normal for Facebook. But thankfully, there weren't many on this one.

"Guys, look at this..." Zach held his phone up to their view.

It was no longer a mystery. Genni was no longer "missing."

22

"Sheriff Mullins had no further statement on the killing of the teenaged Genesis Fisher. The police statement was released on their Facebook page. We're waiting for more information regarding this case. When we have more, we'll come to you with live updates." The newswoman spoke with elegance and was straightforward on the screen. The police station behind her cast a perfect backdrop for the television. Next to her, news stations from every network were talking into microphones with camera crews lined up and down the sidewalk.

The front door opened to reveal Deputy Marie Evans swiftly making her way down the steps to her patrol car. The news crews hurried after her, sticking out their microphones.

"Ma'am!"

"What was the state of her body!?"

"Had Ms. Fisher been in any trouble!?"

"What is the sheriff doing about the situation?!"

Deputy Evans sat in her car after slamming the door. She pulled out onto the road as fast as she could. When she was far enough away, she started to show her true emotions from the new stress that was on the town. It was the day after Christmas, and she was here trying to figure out what happened to Genni and who did it.

She sighed, taking one hand off the steering wheel and rubbing it through her hair.

"Why did you let her out? Why did she have to go out that night!?" Genni's mother yelled at her husband.

"I had no idea! Do you think I wanted this?!" he yelled back at her. The broken dishes, dirty tissues, and holes punched into walls couldn't explain the anger they felt over losing Genni, and it ripped what was left of their relationship apart.

That night was the coldest night so far of the winter. Jasper's thick coat sat at the edge of Natalie's bed. He knew the time was right. Derrick was out of the picture... maybe he could be there for Natalie...

He picked up his camera and took a picture of her. Crossed legs on her blue, plaid bed. Her hair was wavy from the braids she had in all day. Her smile was brighter than ever. Besides everything, she felt liberated. It was maybe time for a new start.

The camera flashed onto her, capturing this moment. He looked down at the picture, smiling and letting his face heat up with blush. She was cute, and he wasn't hiding his feelings anymore. Natalie squinted her eyebrows in confusion.

"Lemme see," she reached forward. The bed creaked as she leaned for the camera.

Jasper turned the screen around to her. "Here," he said with a smile. She grabbed it and hit the zoom button. It was quiet for a second. She was calm, seeing a picture that really showed how she felt. But Jasper, he was about to explode with butterflies.

Do I tell her? I'm gonna tell her. I shouldn't. I can't tell her. Finally, the war in his head was over.

"Natalie…" he started.

"Yeah?" she asked, still looking at the camera.

"I—I love you."

She didn't look away from the camera, thinking it was nothing. "What?" she chuckled.

"I've liked you for years. Derrick's gone, and I'm here for you." He took a deep breath. "I love you."

"Uhh," she handed Jasper his camera and looked down to her bed. "Thanks, Jasper." Her bottom lip started to quiver. He didn't mean to hurt her, but Natalie had been through so much with Derrick… she wasn't ready. "Give me a minute. I'll be back." She stood up from the squeaky bed and went outside, not letting Jasper say a single word.

Jasper stayed on the bed and listened as he heard her car start and pull out of the driveway.

"What the crap was that?" he said in a shaky voice. His nerves were over boiling. "She wants me to sit here? I'm not doing that!"

Out of embarrassment, he stood up from the bed and was ready to leave. He didn't notice the gun sitting under her bed as he walked away. His camera slung down from his shoulder-strap and hit him in the stomach. He passed by the windows in the hallway and stepped outside to his car.

"I don't know what to do," he whispered. He slid his keys into the slot without starting the car. He dropped his camera into the passenger seat and put his head on the steering wheel.

"Why?" he said, lifting his head and banging it on the steering wheel. Without looking up, he rose his hand and switched on the headlights. The lights beamed through the driveway.

"Why did I do that?" he said again, hitting his head on the steering wheel again. Finally, he rose his teary eyes to start the engine. But, standing just a few feet from the car, someone was creating a huge shadow.

The lights shined into the red hoodie, showing their face.

Jasper rolled down the window. "What are you doing?" he asked his friend between his sniffles and shaky voice.

They didn't say a word.

Just silence, a red hoodie, and a crowbar.

23

Jasper leaned out his window. "Hey. What's up?" he yelled.

Silence. The person in the red hoodie walked slowly to the window. Their boots dragging in the gravel. They stopped, looking eye-to-eye with Jasper. They left the crowbar at their side. The darkness made it too hard to see them anymore. The lights from the radio were dimly shining on Jasper's face. Enough to show he wasn't scared... not yet.

"You have to be next. They need to understand."

"What are you talking about?" Jasper asked. Leaning into the window. "Stop being so weird. What's up with you?"

In the darkness, below Jasper's range of sight, they tightened their grip around the crowbar, getting ready to swing. They rose their hand, revealing the crowbar.

"Woah!" Jasper yelled as he jumped back. The crowbar swung through the opening and slammed into the steering wheel. The horn went off as they pulled it back out. Jasper pushed himself into the passenger seat, not caring if he smashed his camera. The shutter clicked, but no flash. He struggled to hit the lock for the doors in the dark. First, he hit the unlock, *click*, then the lock button. He couldn't get his hands to stop shaking.

"Stop! This isn't funny!" he yelled. They leaned in the car window and grabbed the keys that were still in the ignition. Jasper reached as fast as he could to fight for the keys. They dinged against each other as they slipped out of their hands and into the floorboard. The killer reached forward and used this opportunity to grab Jasper's wrist. He leaned back into the cold window of the passenger side and pulled his leg back. He pushed forward a kick to the face as hard as he could.

The red hoodie flopped back as they fell to the ground outside the car. Jasper spilled into the floorboard, searching for the keys. He grabbed them and slammed them into the ignition, staying as far away from the open window as he could. He turned the key, starting the car. He leaned over, trying to hit the gas pedal with his foot. He had to move closer to the open window, and in a flash of an eye, the crowbar came flying into the car.

Spud! It hit him in the arm right below his left shoulder. "AHH!" he yelled. He grabbed the crowbar, still sticking out of his arm. He tried to pull it out as he went for the gas pedal. His foot hit it, making the car's engine screech. He didn't put it in drive.

As he reached for the gear shift, the killer grabbed his head and slammed it into the steering wheel. From the inside, they hit the unlock button on the door. They grabbed the handle and swung the door open. Jasper screamed as he yanked the crowbar out of his arm. Blood shot all over the inside of his car.

He fell out of the car, slinging the crowbar with his good arm, "Get away! Get away from me! Look at what you've done!"

"It wasn't you. This isn't your fault. But it had to be done, Jasper."

"Stop it! Get away from me!" he yelled, pointing the crowbar at the killer. The red hoodie was down, revealing their face.

Jasper reached for his phone with his other arm, but it wasn't strong enough. As he cringed in unbearable pain, he closed his eyes and loosened his tension on the crowbar. The killer lunged forward, knocking him to the ground. The crowbar flung out of his hand as he hit the ground. The killer jumped off Jasper and hurried for the crowbar. Jasper, still screaming in pain, jumped up and ran onto Natalie's porch.

The killer jumped from their knees to their feet as they chased Jasper onto the porch. They hiked up their arms in preparation for a final blow.

Swing. Gush. Crunch. The crowbar slammed into Jasper's back.

"Ahhhhh!" he screamed for his life.

The killer used the leverage from the crowbar in his back to pull him down into the steps of the front porch. He squalled as he turned over and tried crawling for help. The killer stood over his bloody body. They slipped the red hoodie back over their head, rose the crowbar, and slammed it into his neck.

They pulled the crowbar out, letting the blood continue to pour onto the dead grass.

"I'm sorry, Jasper. Maybe now they'll understand."

24

"Please! I can't—I don't know what to—help me!" Natalie yelled at the top of her lungs into the phone. She kept taking deep breaths between her yelling. Tears raced down her face.

"Ma'am, please calm down."

"No! I can't—" she started hyperventilating, "Please—help—me."

"Let me help you, ma'am please calm down. What is your address?"

Her voice was shaking in sync with her hands as she told her the address. She sat in her car, screaming at the phone, too scared to get out. She could see his body just on the ground. Damp in his own blood. Lifeless.

"Ma'am, we're coming. Are you safe?"

Natalie's eyes shot open. She looked down the driveway and around her car. "I think so..." she said between her tears.

"Can you stay on the phone with me?"

Then it hit her...the gun. It was still sitting under her bed. She hung up the phone and dropped it into a cup holder. She stared out the window towards the front porch.

"I have to get it," she whispered.

She tied her hair up with the hair band around her wrist. She popped the door open and ran towards the bloody scene. She passed Jasper's car as she ran toward his body. She didn't look down as she jumped over him, avoiding all the blood along the way. She went around the steps and climbed up on the porch to miss the blood on the steps. She went to her window that she knew was unlocked and propped it open.

She ducked her head and slipped into the heated inside of the house. She dropped to her hands and knees and hurried for the gun under her bed. She reached across the carpet, cheek on the floor, to reach it. She grasped it in her hand and pulled it out. She ran back to her car the same way she came, but this time she looked down. She almost vomited just looking at him. Eyes open, mouth open, blood everywhere. He just told her he loved her, and now he's dead. He's gone. Just like Genni...

She clenched on tighter to the gun, not willing to let go. She scuffled for her car, still trying to avoid any blood from getting on her or her shoes. She didn't need her footprints in the slaying.

She flopped into the driver seat and locked the door. She stared back at Jasper, then looked around the dark outside of the car. She kept checking to make sure the car was locked and that the gun was loaded.

She looked down the driveway anxiously waiting for the cops to arrive.

25

"Listen to me, it's going to be okay, Natalie." Robert's hands were shaking around Natalie's face. He was trying the best he could to keep his cool for his step-daughter, but Jasper's death was wrecking his nerves, too.

"How was—I was just—" Natalie couldn't get anything out. Her eyes were wide, and she was too shocked to let tears roll. She couldn't blink, she couldn't breathe, and she felt like everything was freezing around her. Time didn't feel like it was moving, and she wished she could have gone backward.

Deputy Evans grabbed Robert's shoulder; his gray t-shirt had a few of his tears hiding in the fabric. He turned and looked at her, hoping she would know what to say. Sadly, she had done this before.

"Honey, I'm terribly sorry… and there is nothing I can say or do to fill that hole. I can't make anything better, but it's going to be okay. I'd like to ask you a few questions if I could…"

The red and blue lights were flashing and spinning onto their faces. The cold breeze wasn't even a bother. They didn't even notice their breath forming and becoming visible in the frigid air.

Natalie looked over to Jasper's body one last time as they were being ushered away by Deputy Evans. Steam was forming above Jasper's body from the warm blood. His eyes seemed like they were following her.

I love you, she heard again in her head.

"Don't look, hun." Deputy Evans turned her head away from the ugly scene.

"I loved you too, Jasper," she whispered under her breath.

Kathrine was sitting in her living room next to her Mom, they were watching the screen, anxiously waiting for Sheriff Mullins' new announcement. Fayetteville wasn't ready for another blunt force to the temple.

"We are aware that this is an urgent problem. We've lost another teen close to our hearts in this town of

Fayetteville. Anyone that we lose is a devastating blow to the community," he paused. He looked back at the Director of Communications and the Mayor. They nodded for him to continue.

"It is believed to be connected to the murder of Genesis Fisher," he straightened his hat as he read from the papers on the podium in front of him. The press muttered and leaned in for more. "I understand this may hurt businesses and some establishments, but after consideration with the town administration, we have come to a needed conclusion for the town," he rose up and looked directly into the camera. "I am setting forth a curfew. No one is permitted to be out in the town after 8 p.m."

Kathrine's mom grabbed the remote and turned the television off.

Clink. Clink. Clink. Clink. The metal bars clicked as they passed each other. They rang in place as they created the opening in the holding cell.

Sheriff Mullins emerged from the shadow in the opening. The moonlight from the small window was casting an eerie dark shadow on the right side of his face. "Let's go, son." He didn't look up. "Be careful out there."

Derrick grabbed the bench he was sitting on to prop himself up. He rose up into the moonlight as he made his way out of the holding cell and back out to Fayetteville.

26

Going back to high school after the horrible winter break was bitter sweet. It was something to distract them from the constant traumatic events, but it was school. They were all zoned out in class. Derrick, Kathrine, Zach, Evelyn, and Natalie did everything they could to hold back tears in class. They all had emotions bursting at the seams. They weren't the only ones... every seat was filled with aching hearts and empty notebooks. Everyone wanted to be ready to get back to life, but nobody was able to.

Natalie didn't waste any time between classes and zoomed down the hall in about 30 seconds. She walked into her fourth and final class for the day, sat down, pulled out her phone, and waited for the teacher to start class. The desks around her started to be filled. People would look her way, but no one reached out... not yet.

She saw the one empty seat to the right of her out of the corner of her eye. Then, the blue jeans and hefty green jacket flashed into her line of sight. She knew that jacket. She used to wear it sometimes.

"Natalie…" Derrick said.

"No," she said without looking up. She tapped her foot on the tile to ease the tension. She pivoted in the chair to stay away from him.

At the end of class, right before the bell rang, he slid an unfolded, torn paper over her desk. She looked down, and he was gone before she finished reading it.

i just want you to know i'm sorry

After class, Natalie went back to her blue locker and pushed her backpack inside. She slowly unzipped it, looking behind her to make sure no one was doing what they do best: being nosey.

She reached inside and rubbed her fingers over the handle of her gun. She peeked inside. *Safety's still on*, she thought.

Deputy Evans stepped into Sheriff Mullins' office with a stack of papers. She sat down in front of him as the sheriff dropped his hat from his head to his desk.

"So, we went through Jasper's camera like you asked. I think these might be helpful…" she said as she slid them over his hat and closer to his side of the desk.

He spread the photos out over his messy desk.

The first one was a photo of someone in a red hoodie walking down a sidewalk at night. The Coca-Cola mural told him it was on the square in town.

The next photo was of Natalie on her bed. The timestamp on the photo was just a few minutes before his death.

And the third… a photo of the inside of Jasper's car. In the open door, someone in a red hoodie was reaching in, but Jasper's leg was covering their face in the frame.

"That's him…" she told him. "That's the killer."

27

Zach shoved his face deeper into his pillow. He squeezed the ends of the dark blue pillow case until he almost ripped it apart. He leaned up, tears rolling down his face, grinding his teeth in anger; he slammed his fist into the pillow.

"No!" he yelled. Over and over again. As if he could beat his pillow into making Jasper come back. He lost another friend... all over again.

Evelyn's shadow emerged in his bedroom door. He leaned up, but his tears still blurred his vision. He could see her silhouette change to her wiping her face, too. A sniffle broke the silence.

"Me too, Zach," she whispered between her tears. She made her way over his dirty clothes and untied shoes to sit on his bed. Zach leaned up to meet her, leaning on her shoulder.

"Who would do this? Why Jasper?" he asked.

Her hands were shaking, and she took a deep breath to hold back her tears. "I have no idea... if I knew, I would do anything to stop them. But I'm scared that this is so much bigger than we think."

"It's bigger than we are... it's bigger than I am..." he whispered.

"What?" she asked.

"I can't do this, Evelyn. How are we supposed to be okay? How do we continue?"

"We have to... I know, I don't want to either... but we have to."

"Continue until we're next?" He closed his eyes and let another tear fall onto his gray bed sheets.

Kathrine leaned down, letting her towel drop over her shoulders. She grabbed the sheep-white towel and spun it around her hair. She flipped it up on top of her head to let it soak in the rest of the hot water in her hair. She ran her hand over the fogged mirror to reveal her face. The water ran down over the mirror to the sink. *Drip*. The shower was still draining.

Her phone was sitting on the counter's edge next to the sink. The song that was playing changed into something more relatable. The songs that put you in a bad mood, but it's so relatable that you have to listen to it. Thinking you could have written the lyrics yourself.

I think I'm done

Trying to run from the gun

But I feel like I have to

Can I run where there is no sun

The depressing tones and beats bounced between the moist and steamy walls of the bathroom. Kathrine felt like she had done nothing but run her entire life. She had her mom, but she was forcing her to run with her. She had to... she was her mom. She ran to Tennessee to get away from Florida.

Where to next? She thought it was time to pack her bags and get out again.

Her phone lit up. She leaned down and read the message. She almost dropped her phone with her wet hands, but she opened it, letting her nerves get the best of her. Her hands started shaking as the messages rolled in.

You thought you could just run...??

Well we found you, fattie

Don't think about running again

I would get a lawyer. You'll be back here soon

The messages kept rolling in. She didn't know how to respond...

Stop it!

Who is this??

Once again, he shuffled his papers. He stepped up to the podium ready to talk to his town. This time, behind the sheriff was Deputy Evans and two FBI agents. He was ready to give as much information to Fayetteville as he could. He wanted to protect his people, and he felt like giving what he could to the press would be helpful.

After Sheriff Mullins gave his speech, he used just the right words for the news outlets to turn it into a catchphrase. There's the Zodiac Killer from California, the Phantom Killer from Texarkana; it didn't take but three hours before all the major news networks shared the term. They showed the picture Jasper took on the square of the person in the hoodie walking down the sidewalk. That was the famous picture.

But nobody was saying "the person in the hoodie." Everyone in the news made a term that would never be forgotten, and everyone in Fayetteville would hate that color for the rest of its existence... or at least until they figured out the identity.

The killer finally had a name: *RED*.

28

Kathrine didn't even let herself think. She didn't know what to do. She stared at the phone's screen like it had her in a hypnotic trance. She couldn't stop the bright pixels from seeping into her brain. She slid the name to the left and hit delete.

Gone. The messages were gone... but the truth wasn't. Yes, Kathrine was running from what happened in Florida, but it was chasing her.

"His funeral was awful. They didn't do him justice! You know that?" Natalie said, hitting her steering wheel in the parking lot of the high school after classes let out. Her car was next to Evelyn's and it was one of the last few there.

"I know... He was such a good person. He grew up dealing with so much, but he didn't let any of it stop him. He never gave up..." Evelyn turned the vent away from her. It was freezing outside, but Natalie's temperature was boiling. She was blasting the AC. "I wasn't as close to him, but I know you were… and I haven't gotten to tell you this yet. I just want you to know how sorry I am. I couldn't imagine what you're dealing with. I miss him. I'm terribly sad. But, he wasn't my best friend like he was to you."

Natalie lost it. It was more than tears; snot and saliva were covering her face in spite of her effort to wipe it away.

She took a deep breath. "I don't think he was just my best friend. I took him for granted. Derrick wasn't right for me… Jasper was. And he told me—" she bolted out a cry.

Evelyn let her catch her breath again.

Natalie turned to her, showing her bloodshot eyes resting in dark circles. The AC was the only sound roaring in the car. "He told me he loved me right before— I left him alone. I was there and walked out."

"It could have been you," Evelyn said.

"I didn't even think of that. I didn't even care. What's crazy is that I left him alone… just like he had spent his life. *Alone*. And what's even more twisted… I think I loved him, too."

"Natalie, I'm—" Evelyn started to try to comfort her, but Natalie cut her off.

118

"No. I have to go," she said as she popped the locks open on the car.

"If you need anything—"

"Please."

Evelyn reached down and pulled the handle. She stepped out into the brisk air and got into her car. Natalie pulled out of the parking lot as soon as she closed the door. She took a left at the light, headed toward the police station.

Kathrine sat in the coffee house at the wooden table in the far-right corner of the building. She spun her phone on the table by her index finger. Then, she opened it and pulled down on her 'Messages' screen to make sure there weren't any more of those invasive text bubbles. She was constantly checking even when she knew she deleted them.

You here? Zach texted her from the parking lot. They were about to get hot chocolate together. Somehow, in the middle of all these emotions, he still had butterflies. *Those* butterflies.

29

"Why, though?" Kathrine asked Zach. There weren't any other noises in the coffee shop beside the clinking of mugs behind the counter as the barista cleaned up. She was lowering her voice even though the barista couldn't hear them.

"I can't really pinpoint what it is. Maybe your looks, but there's so much more to you. The way you're finding a place here in Fayetteville is something I want. I mean, I hate you came here in the middle of all this, but I'm glad you're here, Kathrine."

She started to blush. This conversation was actually making her forget about the messages she had received. Zach was showing interest in her... and she was showing it back.

"Well, I can't say I expected to be here and all that stuff happen. I didn't expect to lose two of my first friends... I didn't expect to be there when..." she dropped her head. She was still trying to keep the night of Genni's death out of her mind, but it was back.

"Hey," he leaned towards the table and wrapped his hand around hers. His warmth and her cold met in the middle to a normal temperature. She looked up from the floor and their eyes met. Chemistry. They could feel it.

"I'm sorry I freaked out on you that night in the dark before we found Derrick's crowbar."

"What? Oh, I forgot about that. Don't sweat it," he smiled. His shadow of a beard parted to show his shining teeth. Somehow, his dimples still peeked through, too.

Kathrine smiled back and squeezed his hand one final time before letting go. She pulled her hand away and off the table.

Zach picked up his mug to finish his hot chocolate, but he had already finished it. He set it back on the table right as the barista made his way to them.

"I just want to let you guys know that we're closing in about ten minutes. Would you like anything else?" he asked.

"No, I think we're good. I have to head home," Kathrine told him.

They both stood up and pushed their chairs into the table. They walked towards the door together, and Zach's finger hit her hand. He went ahead and wrapped his hand around hers again.

He looked back toward the barista. "Thank you!"

At her car, he leaned in for a hug, but the butterflies in his stomach wouldn't let him go in for a kiss. But Kathrine wouldn't of let him, even if he tried. She learned that lesson from Derrick.

"Bye, Zach," she whispered as she reached for the handle of the car.

Buzz. Her phone vibrated in her pocket. Her heart stopped. She fell into the driver seat and unlocked her phone.

We're pressing charges soon.

Get a lawyer

You're done, Fathrine.

"Fathrine." One of the words that started it all.

That's not my name, she texted back.

Could've fooled me, they responded.

As Kathrine made her way back into her house, she moved extra slow and ignored the cold. She was thinking...

122

was it really about to hit the fan? Was she really going to have to go back to Florida to settle this? She thought it was over. She thought she had gotten away without a trace...

Her mom was watching the television with a bag of delicious-smelling, extra-butter popcorn.

"Mom..." she whispered. "I need to tell you something..."

30

"Sit down, honey," Kathrine's mom turned the television off and patted on the space next to her on the couch.

Kathrine dropped her head and rubbed her sweaty palms together. She tried to rub it off onto her jeans but her nerves were getting the best of her.

"You have to promise not to be mad at me…"

"I can't promise that, Kat. You need to tell me what you did. I'm here for you…"

Kathrine let the memories rush back. All the things they said. All the things they did to her. She wasn't those things they called her. She didn't deserve the things they did to her… then she took matters into her own hands.

"Remember those people that wouldn't leave me alone… they wouldn't leave *us* alone."

"I won't forget them, Kat. I can't."

"I wanted to get back at them... so I took their pets. Their sweet dog, one of their cats, and really anything I could get my hands on."

"So, you stole their pets?" her mom looked at the ceiling with her eyebrows scrunched together. "I'm confused... Why are you telling me this now?"

"I killed their pets. All of them."

Kathrine's mom let go of her hand. "Why did you do that? That's not okay, Kathrine."

"I did more than that, Mom..."

She didn't respond. She just ran her fingers over the plaid couch fabric. *What did my daughter do?* she thought.

"I fed their pets to them," Kathrine stared at the ground. She was filled with shame, but it used to be pride.

"You... fed these bullies their own pets? Like, they ate their own pets?" There were so many questions. "What? Why?... How did you do this? How did they just now find out?"

"I think Heather told them. She knew and helped me take one of the pets. She had the cookout at her house and I replaced the meat with their pets. She knew I did it, but she turned a blind eye. She felt sorry for me, and she helped me. She must have told them." Kathrine stuck her fingers into her pocket and slipped her phone onto the couch. "Here."

"Kathrine... this is beyond twisted. This is too far. I know they bullied you. They made you want to end it all... but that was *wrong,* and you're about to pay for it."

"I don't want to go back," she hid her face. Her tears dropped to the couch from behind her hands.

"We have to... but I'm going with you. I'll never turn my back on you," she leaned in and held her daughter the way any mother should.

Fayetteville was closing up. Curfew was just minutes away before the cops would come and patrol the small-town streets searching for RED. This town was ready to fight back. They wanted to do whatever it took to stay safe.

RED had caused a new sense of fear in every household in the town. Genni's father sat in his truck in the parking lot behind McDonald's. He couldn't keep his eyes off anyone walking by. He never thought he would catch RED, but he would do whatever he could.

With tears still in his eyes, he reached into the glove box and put the pistol on his lap. He leaned back in hopes that RED would come to him. So he could fling the hoodie of their head and pull the trigger himself.

The Thompson boy fumbled his keys in the air as he made his way to his car. When he found Genni's body in the river with his dad, he thought he'd never be the same. He had nightmares about that day in the cold river... he even thought about seeing a counselor.

He wasn't thinking when he left his house to go to the store... Why that hoodie? Why today?

Genni's father popped the door open and stormed over the yellow parking spaces to meet him at his car.

"*Hey!*" he yelled.

He looked up, letting his face hit the light. His red hoodie flopped back to reveal his identity. If only Genni's dad knew who this kid was and what he had done for the Fisher family. This boy found his daughter...

"Hey?" he said. "Ummm, can I help you?"

"Yeah, you can, actually."

Genni's dad rose the pistol from the inside of his jacket, set the boy in his aim, and pulled the trigger.

31

"That wasn't me that was shot. I'm still here."

"I'm sorry... who is this?"

"I like the name you gave me," they chuckled into the burner phone.

"I didn't catch your name..."

"You'll see why I'm doing this. I'm not stopping."

The nervous secretary in the police station waved at Deputy Evans. She ran to the desk and hit speaker. "Can you please state your name?"

"*RED.*"

Click.

The secretary looked at Deputy Evans. Her eyebrows were raised in not only confusion but also shock. "What do we do?"

Deputy Evans leaned up and nodded to Sheriff Mullins as he approached the desk.

❖ ❖ ❖

Kathrine and her mom grabbed their bags out of the airport and shuffled into the taxi cab. The air was warmer than what they had gotten used to in Tennessee. Kathrine and her mom were always talking, but this time they were together in silence. She didn't know exactly what to say. It was like the burden of what she had done was pulling her underwater. She couldn't talk. She could barely breathe.

Finally, she could get something out. "How long will we be here?"

"I'm not expecting it to be too long. Maybe a week? We'll see." Her mom scratched her elbow in a nervous tick and strung her hair into a ponytail. "When we get to the hotel you need to change quickly. We don't have long before we see the lawyer."

Zach sat in his room waiting on Kathrine to text him back. He was anxiously waiting to see her name pop up on his phone. He'd get those butterflies like that night at the coffee shop just from seeing her name.

He was beginning to let the crush grow. He was letting his walls finally come down. After his parent's divorce, he didn't want the hurt to come and invade his life anymore... easier said than done.

You're nervous, Evelyn texted him from her bedroom.

No I'm not, he sent back.

You're clicking the pen you're holding so loud that it's driving me crazy.

Put in headphones, he joked with her.

He threw the pen onto his desk. It landed on his homework he should have started hours ago.

Someone's at the door, Evelyn sent.

Answer it

No. You do it. I'm tired and lazy lol

His fidgeting energy transferred into sweaty hands as he went to the front door. He wasn't nervous about answering it, but Kathrine was still on his mind.

He grabbed the knob and pulled the front door open. Zach's eyes shot open.

"Hey…" Derrick said.

32

"Can I come in..." Derrick shuffled his hands into his denim pockets.

"Uh," Zach ran his index finger over the back of the door. "Yeah... you can."

"Thanks," Derrick reached for a handshake. Zach stepped back and let him walk in without even looking at his hand.

Derrick nodded as he stepped inside. He wasn't expecting a warm welcome. He turned and leaned against the loveseat he had pushed Zach over just a few weeks ago. He pulled his hat off and set it on his knee. Zach shut the door behind him; he started to grab the lock then thought better of it.

"I know I've messed up. I know I've made everything worse. I've done my time, and I thought that you deserved an apology. You've been there for me until I blew up... I wouldn't let anyone be there for me. I just want you to know I'm trying."

"Trying won't cut it, Derrick." Zach crossed his arms.

"And that's fine. I don't think I deserve to be accepted again. I've dug a hole and I fell in it. I don't expect anyone to hop down with me and help me up."

"It's not that, Derrick. You freaking hit Natalie! You have caused so much hurt. You have been nothing but a problem. You know that?" he screamed.

"Yes, I know," he said. He ran his fingers through his hair, and he couldn't look up at Zach.

"Jasper's gone…"

"I know. I'm still trying to get past—"

"No, *we're* trying. That's the problem. You never saw yourself as the part of our group." He started pointing at him. "You were worried about *yourself* all this time. And, I'm surprised you're out."

Derrick swiped a tear away just as it slipped from his eye. He was trying to hide it.

"We thought it was you. Then Jasper was—" Zach couldn't finish the sentence. "You were locked up. So, it wasn't you…"

134

It was hurting Zach to be like this. He was trying his best to hold back the tears. He thought of the times they played video games together until 4 a.m. on the weekends. He thought about the time he cried on Derrick's shoulder when his parents got the divorce.

"I'm here for you, Derrick," his voice was shaky. "I believe in second chances... I'm sure I'll need a second chance someday."

Derrick met eyes with Zach. "I'm sorry, man." His voice was shakier than Zach's. He could feel the horrible feeling in his throat from trying to hold it back. He was sorry, and he meant it.

He stuck out his hand one last time. Zach reached forward, let a tear drop, and shook his hand.

33

Derrick left Zach and Evelyn's house feeling comfort. He wasn't expecting to fix anything; he just wanted to apologize. He actually had a genuine smile for the first time in months. He sat in the driver seat and said a thankful prayer before turning his engine on and pulling away.

Zach turned to go down the hallway back to his room, but Evelyn was standing in the way, leaning against the corner.

"Well, dang," she chuckled.

"What?" Zach laughed between his sniffles.

"Derrick actually apologized? What's gotten into him!?" she joked.

"I know," he smiled. "Maybe things are turning around." He walked closer to the hallway, but Evelyn didn't move.

"Don't trust him, Zach. I'm not going to lose you to him."

"He's not RED."

"We don't know who RED is... just be careful, please."

Natalie was screaming in her room and yanking at her hair. She could barely be there knowing Jasper was just sitting on her bed. He told her he loved her, and then his body sat outside. She hated the house and was ready to leave. She lunged off her bed and grabbed her keys off the nightstand. She slung the door back, making the handle slam into the wall and leave a dent.

"Baby, what's wrong," her mom asked from the kitchen as she passed.

"I can't do this!" she screamed and ran for the door.

Her mom leaned against the counter. She knew Natalie better than anyone and knew she would be okay. She needed her time. She let her tears fall and said her prayers.

Natalie was so frazzled that she didn't take the car out of park before she slammed on the gas.

Bruuuuun. The engine yelled.

She slammed the gear shift into drive and pulled out of the driveway.

She couldn't control anything. It all just slipped from her fingers like a balloon into the sky. She couldn't wipe at her nose enough to keep the snot away. The high beams shined through the night, knowing she would be pulled over for even being out after curfew. She didn't even have enough control to care.

The last thing she lost control of was her foot. It kept pressing down.

Faster. Faster. Even faster. The needle on the dash was inching its way to the red section as the speed kept increasing to levels the car had never gone before.

"*Ahhhhhh*!" she screamed. She squalled in tears. There wasn't much of anything left in her. Static.

Derrick flashed in her head. The way he threw her from the porch. Jasper. The love. The death. The gun.

Blue lights... but this wasn't in her head. She slammed on her breaks and pulled over into the gravel section of the road. The gravel popped and moved under her tires and Deputy Evans followed behind her. After stopping, she stepped from the patrol car. She had one hand on her gun and the other holding the flashlight.

Natalie's gun was sitting just in the darkness by her knee on the center cupholder. She moved it to the floorboard as the flashlight hit her shoulders from behind.

Deputy Evans looked through the window from an angle, making sure to keep her distance. The blue and red lights still flashing around as bright as they could, they were blinding Natalie from her rearview mirror.

Natalie knew if Deputy Evans were to find the gun, she would be in trouble... more than she wanted to be in. She looked back and met eyes with Deputy Evans.

34

"You're not supposed to be out, ma'am," Deputy Evans told her, keeping her flashlight shining in her face.

"Yep," Natalie said, short and sweet. Her leg was bouncing in and out of the light; she couldn't make it stop.

Deputy Evans leaned in, trying to inspect the inside of her car. If she tilted the flashlight just right, it would expose the gun in her floorboard.

Natalie didn't look up; her eyes were glued on the road where she wanted to keep going. She wanted to keep running, but she couldn't. Maybe Deputy Evans saved her life that night, or maybe someone else's...

After Evans took her license back to the patrol car, she ran it through the identification system. When her face popped on the screen, she remembered it. She remembered the nasty scene sitting right beside the steps to the front porch. *Jasper was killed at this girl's house*, she thought.

Was Natalie this upset that she was running? Was she trying to get away?

Or was the fact that the death happened at her house more than a coincidence?

That night, Deputy Evans had something else on her mind... she came back to Natalie's car and made a choice.

"I remember you, Natalie. I'm really sorry. But, this isn't safe, and there isn't an excuse," Deputy Evans handed the driver's license back through the window. "I'm going to escort you home. Okay?"

"Thank you," Natalie cried.

"Yes, ma'am. She can't run out and do what she wants. It's curfew," Deputy Evans told Natalie's mom.

"She's really struggling... and we're looking for a new house. We can't be here. It's horrible. We can't even walk through the front door..." Pam, Natalie's mom, took her glasses off and placed them on the counter. "I don't know what to do..."

"Be there for her," Deputy Evans turned toward the door. The ring of keys on her hip dangled in the silence. She stopped at the door. "I have to go, but she's a good kid. Don't let her lose it…"

"I'm afraid," Pam whispered.

"We all are…" Deputy Evans said. She reached for the door handle and turned the knob.

"Thank you for being here for me," Deputy Evans told Sheriff Mullins. They were sitting on her front porch swing. The few chirping birds were starting to come out as the pink, orange sunrise was coming up over the hill.

"You don't have to thank me," he reached up and placed his arm around her. "I want to be here, Marie."

"That's Deputy Evans to you, sir," she chuckled.

"Hey! I'm the sheriff here!" he smiled.

For a moment, everything was in the back of their minds. RED didn't exist. Jasper, Genni, and the boy in the parking lot were still alive. They forgot about all the horrible things that had been happening in Fayetteville.

Deputy Evans turned from the sunrise and towards the sheriff. Their eyes met, and then closed. Their lips touched, transferring their warmth on the cold morning.

Deputy Marie Evans pulled away. "Is this wrong?" she asked.

"I don't care," he told her as he leaned in for another kiss.

35

"That boy was stupid for wearing the jacket. Why would you wear a red hoodie in this town?" the high school student said as she stepped out of the building and under the balcony toward the parking lot.

"Hey, he had a name!" someone snapped from across the crowd.

"Mind your own business, faggot," she chirped back at him.

Evelyn was walking out next to "the faggot." All she could think about was Jasper. He was always called the same thing, and Evelyn wasn't going to just let this happen anymore. She reached forward and grabbed the boy's arm.

"Hey, don't listen to her. You're not what she just called you," she turned her shoulders toward the girl making her way through the parking lot. "Watch your mouth! Don't call him that!"

"What are you going to do about it!?" she yelled as she flopped into the passenger seat of her friend's truck.

Evelyn turned back to the guy as more students poured out of the school around them. "I'm sorry, man," she hugged him, and she didn't even know his name.

Behind them, Natalie was bumping her way to the front of the crowd. She was ready to get out of there. She tightened the straps on her backpack and nudged someone next to her. She stepped off the sidewalk and into the parking lot.

"Watch it," they snapped at her.

She didn't even acknowledge them as she kept moving to her car. They probably wouldn't have said that if they knew Natalie had a loaded gun in her bag… and Derrick probably wouldn't have been leaning against her car in the freezing cold if he knew what she had, either.

"Hey," he gently whispered as she approached her car.

She slung her bag off her shoulders and dangled it in front of her.

"Don't beg for me, Derrick. Move," she demanded without any emotion on her pale face.

"I'm not here to ask you to come back to me. I'm here to apologize. Face to face, I wanted you to know I'm sorry." He saw Evelyn walking to her car behind Natalie. He wanted to wave, but he hadn't apologized to her yet... *hopefully soon*, he thought.

Natalie unzipped her bag and reached inside. The keys were sitting right beside the loaded gun. "Are you... *really* sorry, Derrick?"

"You know me, Nat. I'm not going to say sorry if I'm not."

Natalie didn't believe him, and she wrapped her hand around the handle of the pistol hidden in her bag.

"That's all, Nat. I'm sorry," he said as he perched up from the car and turned to walk away.

He walked away feeling happy. He was proud that he apologized, and he hoped Natalie received it well. If he only knew how close she was to pulling the gun out of the bag and letting all of her anger and frustration out on him right there in the busy, loud, crowded parking lot.

She loosened her grip on the gun and grabbed her keys.

36

"She'll love this," Evelyn said under her breath as she leaned away from her memo board she made Natalie. She knew Natalie was going through way more than she could handle, and she wanted to make her feel loved. It had pictures and memories of all the great times they have had together. From laughing in a photo booth to being kicked out of the park for being too loud too late.

She slid it into the floor of her trunk and dropped a blanket over it. Next to it was a basket of all of Natalie's favorite foods. A nice little care package made with everything to make Natalie smile. But, Evelyn made sure not to include anything with the color red in it.

She sat in the driver seat with her messages open on her phone. She was going to message and make sure Nat was home, but if she wasn't, she would just leave it on the front porch.

I'm coming home soon. Kathrine texted Zach from Florida.

I can't wait to see you, he responded.

Are you okay? he asked her.

Yes. It went better than expected. There was a hole in their story. but I don't want to talk about it.

That's okay. I just want to see you.

Hey! Come outside. I'm in your driveway! Evelyn texted Natalie.

A minute later, the front door creaked open as Natalie hit the switch for the front porch lights. Evelyn jumped out into the cold and moved her way up the steps to hug her. Natalie's matching pajamas were fuzzy and felt like a worn pillowcase.

"I got you something!" Evelyn chirped.

Natalie didn't respond. She just looked around in the darkness; her eyes rocked back and forth. The paranoia wasn't just on her mind, but it was starting to run through her veins. She looked down and silently jumped. Jasper's body flashed in her head. His steaming blood on the ground. She shook her head, ran her finger over the cold pistol sticking out of the back of her pajamas and made her way to Evelyn's car.

"Now, it's nothing big, but I think it could make a difference. I know this whole thing has been hard on you, and I want you to have this," she said.

But Natalie didn't hear a word. She just kept looking over her shoulder as Evelyn opened the trunk of her car.

"Here it is," Evelyn lunged forward to keep Natalie from seeing... but she dropped it and made another quick move into the trunk. If only the basket hadn't slipped. If only the lunge forward didn't trigger a wave of emotions in Natalie.

"*No!*" she screamed. Natalie stepped back, in pure terror. Evelyn's simple move set her off... she reached back and grabbed the pistol and didn't even aim. She pointed it at Evelyn and pulled the trigger as fast as she could.

37

"Robert, wake up!" Pam, Natalie's mom, shoved his tattooed arm.

"Huh, what?" he tried to open his eyes. "What's going on?" he asked.

"I just heard a gunshot. I think it was Natalie..." she jumped from the bed and slid on her slippers. The green fuzz was barely hanging on from how worn they were.

"Natalie? Why?" he asked, still confused as he tried to wake up.

"The gun you gave her!" she shouted.

Robert didn't say a word. He jumped up and threw on his clothes as fast as he could. He hit the doorframe of the bedroom and leaned into the kitchen and dining room area. Evelyn's headlights were still shining through the windows in the kitchen. They acted like a spotlight in Robert's eyes.

Pam yanked her robe off a hanger and raced past Robert. She bumped into the counter as she made her way to the door, but she almost didn't feel it. Her attention was strictly on getting outside.

Evelyn's car was sitting in the driveway. The headlights were shining in Pam's face, and the trunk was open. Natalie was standing away from the trunk, staring at the ground behind the car. The gun was sitting on the ground at her feet in the dusty gravel. Her heavy breath was still rising in the air and mixing with the cold.

"Natalie!" Pam yelled. "What's happening, baby?" She ran down the steps as she held her robe together. "Natalie, honey," she tried to hold back her nerves. She was scared but didn't want Natalie to notice. But Natalie probably wouldn't notice... even if she tried.

When she got to Natalie she grabbed her. "Baby, what's happening?" She hugged the motionless Natalie. As she pulled away, she turned to look behind the trunk.

Evelyn's body was on the ground. She was on her side, with her elbow up in the air. Blood was slowly spilling out into the grass.

"Evelyn!" Pam gasped.

Robert ran up and kicked the pistol away from Natalie. "Get back!" he yelled. He bent over and touched Evelyn's shoulder. "Can you breathe?" he asked.

"Yes," Evelyn moaned through her agony and tears. Her hand was over the bullet wound but it was shaking too much to help anything.

Robert turned to Pam. "Call the police."

Pam jumped up and grabbed Natalie by her elbows. "Why did you do this? Was she going to hurt you?" she desperately asked. She didn't care to show her daughter she was scared anymore. She was crying. Her breath in the air was mixing with Natalie's.

"RED," Natalie whispered.

"Was she going to hurt you?!" Pam screamed.

"I don't think so," Natalie put her hands over her mouth in realization. "No!" she yelled. Her saliva strung from her mouth and into her hands. Her tears came and didn't stop... Not even when Pam called the police.

As the police pulled into Natalie's driveway once again, Pam grabbed Robert with her shaking hands. "You know they're taking her to jail..."

152

"I know," he cried.

38

The hospital monitor above Evelyn's head beeped in tune with her heartbeat. The wires connected to her were intimidating, like a robot morphing to her body. She was awake, but she slept as much as she could. Her parents were in and out of the room, but Zach couldn't visit her as much. He knew Evelyn would be okay, and he wanted to be there with Kathrine when she arrived.

Knock. Knock.

Derrick's knuckles softly bounced on the glass door behind the tan curtain. Evelyn's mom looked up from her old, open book.

Derrick nodded and rose his hand. "Is it alright if I—"

Evelyn's mom propped up from the leather chair. "Yeah, I'll give you a minute." She closed the book but kept her finger on the page she was on. "It's Derrick, right?"

"Yes, ma'am," he smiled.

"I'll be in the hall," she said as she ducked behind the curtain.

He looked up at the machines above Evelyn's head. The blue and green lights seemed to be a good thing. She's alive, at least.

"Hey, Derrick," she slid her eyes open.

"I'm so sorry this happened, Ev," he leaned against the wall in front of her. He moved next to the whiteboard so he didn't erase anything.

"Hey! It could be worse," she tried to laugh.

"Yes, it could..." he looked at the floor.

"Your girl shot me, man!" she chuckled, holding her side.

"She's not my girl," he laughed. "I can't believe she shot you... what's happening to this town?"

"Yeah, I know. I'm trying to stay positive," she smiled.

"I don't know if I could say the same if I was shot," he pointed at her wound. "If anybody ever wants to shoot me, they better aim and get it done in one shot."

"You're a mess, boy," she joked again.

"Hey! I'm working on it," he leaned forward and tapped her footboard.

"… Yeah, I've noticed… I don't think you'd be here if you weren't."

He paused. "I *am* sorry, Evelyn."

"What is this? An apology tour?"

"You and your jokes," he chuckled and rolled his eyes.

"I saw you talking to Natalie in the parking lot. Is that why she shot me!?"

He rubbed his hands over his cheeks in embarrassment. "Man, I hope not."

"I'm just messing with you."

He paused and looked back at the floor. "I'm sorry, Evelyn. I really am."

"Come here," she opened her arms the best she could.

Derrick leaned in and gave her a warm hug in the cold hospital room.

"Now, go finish your apology tour!" She let go of him.

156

"Hush it," he joked as he made his way back out of the hospital room. He nodded at Evelyn's mom right outside the glass door. But, he couldn't help but notice that her finger didn't move from that spot in her book. She didn't read a word out there. She was just leaning at the opening in the door.

She stared and watched Derrick as he walked down the hall and turned the corner.

39

"Oh my gosh, I'm so glad you're back," Zach said as he squeezed Kathrine on her front porch. He was sitting on her steps waiting for her to get back.

"Me too... that was a bunch of bull to deal with. I never want to go back to Florida," she told him. Kathrine's mom flipped on the porch light from inside the house.

Zach's body shivered, and his teeth chattered. "Um, can we go in," he said as he rubbed his arms.

"Yeah! Please!" Kathrine laughed.

"Let me," Zach reached for her suitcase and grabbed the denim handle.

Kathrine's mom was putting her dirty clothes in the washer in the laundry room on the other side of the kitchen. "You kids have school in the morning. Don't stay up too late." She closed the washer door. "Throw your dirty clothes in there, baby."

"Goodnight, Mom."

"I love you, Kathrine." She pulled her forward and kissed her on the forehead. "Goodnight, Zach!" she said as she turned down the hall. As she passed, she turned off the kitchen light and turned on the lamp.

"Here you go." Zach sat the heavy suitcase on the couch.

"Oh, you're not taking it to my bedroom?" she said.

"I mean I can," he said cautiously. He wasn't sure what she was hinting at.

"Nah, I got it," she chuckled and hit the suitcase.

"Oh, okay," he started to blush behind his beard.

Kathrine looked into the mirror above the couch and put her hair up into a messy bun. "Evelyn's okay, right?"

Zach had almost forgotten about his step-sister being in the hospital because this beautiful girl in front of him was finally home. "Oh! Yeah, she's going to make it. Last I heard she was in good spirits."

"That's good. I plan on going to see her after school tomorrow," she walked closer to Zach. "How's Natalie? The cops took her?"

"She was arrested... I don't know what's going to happen."

"Do you think she's RED?" Kathrine picked at her nails.

"I... don't think so..." he scratched his neck. The butterflies were back, spinning and rumbling in his stomach.

"I'm sorry. I shouldn't have asked that," she stepped back. "Do you want to come with me to see Evelyn tomorrow?" she changed the subject.

"Yeah, I'll come with you." His thoughts were bouncing all over the place.

"I'll see you tomorrow, Zach." She leaned in and gave him a kiss on the cheek. Then, his lips.

40

"I understand you were scared, Natalie... but you shot her," Sheriff Mullins sat his hat on the interrogation room table once again.

"I know I shot her," she snapped at him.

"Your intention was to kill her, correct?" he asked knowing the answer, but not wanting to hear it. He knew her life was falling apart, and sadly, the shooting was from that.

"Technically... yes. I was trying to kill her."

Sheriff Mullins leaned up and grabbed his hat. He pointed it at her. "But, you were doing it for self-defense." He put his hat back on his head. "I understand, Natalie."

"I'm sorry, brother," Derrick's bottom lip was quivering from trying to hold back his tears. But, it didn't matter... he thought he was alone in the cemetery.

"I love you, man. I'm sorry this happened to you," the floodgates opened. Tears. Snot.

The stress and grief hit Derrick faster than he could process. His stress was boiling over... but this time, it wasn't selfish anger. It was compassionate hurting. He knew he was at rock bottom, and he was losing everyone he ever cared for; he just didn't know how to show it.

"It's going to get better," someone said behind him.

He jolted around, not hiding his emotions. "I didn't see you there," he said.

"Rock bottom sucks... but it's where you learn how to keep going."

Derrick didn't know how to respond, so he leaned up and sat on the concrete bench at Jasper's grave.

"My son was murdered fifteen years ago," he leaned over and grabbed Derrick's shoulder. "You have to keep going."

Genni's dad ran through the cold, dead woods. The leaves crunched under every heavy step. He disregarded it all.

His wife. His life... *everything*. The only thing that mattered was his daughter was gone. He didn't care that he killed an innocent boy for simply wearing a red hoodie. It didn't matter... and he wasn't stopping until Genni's killer was gone.

He ran up to the one-room cabin in the deep woods of Fayetteville. The frigid breeze bit at his fingertips and made the pistol in the back of his pants hurt as it hit his bare skin. He stepped onto the wooden porch and stepped inside. A map of Genni's friends was nailed to the back wall.

He wanted revenge and was determined to get it... but the last thing Fayetteville needed was another killer.

41

"Why don't you even try anymore, Danny!?" Genni's mom yelled.

"I am doing more than you know," he told his wife.

"You're a *pig*, and I would still have *my* daughter if you had done more." She slammed her empty whiskey glass on the dining room table.

"Shut up," Danny, Genni's dad, jumped up from the table. "You get out of my house!"

"No!" She threw the whiskey glass on the floor, letting it shatter like their relationship after Genni's body was found. "You get out of *my* house!" she yelled back him.

Danny threw his hands up. He stood up from the table and grabbed his heavy jacket from the back of the chair. He didn't say a word as he passed the fireplace on the way to the door. He looked back at Genni's photo above the fireplace. The wooden frame surrounded her smiling face. The burning candle bounced light off the photo. He stared one last time...

"For you, Genni... For you, Steven."

He turned and left it all behind, his wife, his house, everything. But he had somewhere to go... he would make the one-room cabin home.

Derrick sat at home in his room with his laptop shining onto his face. His eyes bounced a beautiful color back, and his eyebrows were squished closer together as he typed into the search bar. He wanted more information. Who was that guy in the cemetery?

Fayetteville, TN boy murdered 2000, he typed into Google.

The results shot onto the screen. A few suggested searches sat at the top of the website. He leaned in closer to the bright screen, and one word stuck out. Something seemed... too familiar.

Steven Fisher

"How can we help you?" the carhop at the drive-in restaurant asked from the speaker. The smell of fresh fries and burgers moved from the gray building to the cars in the stalls.

"I want a double cheeseburger and a medium order of fries," Sheriff Mullins said.

"And a milkshake for me," Deputy Evans whispered from the passenger seat.

He turned to the speaker, "Add a chocolate milkshake to that for me," he added.

"Thanks," Deputy Evans whispered.

He leaned over and grabbed her hand. "No problem." He smiled.

Deputy Evans wasn't taking the smile; something else was on her mind. It hadn't stopped racing. "We have to dig deeper... we need help, Jimmy."

"I know we do—" he paused, knowing exactly what she meant.

"These kids are going too soon. Something has to be done," she rubbed her forehead.

"The curfew was a joke... it didn't stop anything," he shrugged his shoulders. "I knew it wouldn't... but I had to do something."

"Something weird is going on with those kids... that friend group."

"Who?" he asked.

"Jasper and Genni's friends... they're so involved in this. I don't think it's all innocent..."

"Here you go!" the carhop handed the food through the window after trading the receipt for the money.

Knock, knock.

"Hey, Mr. Fisher..." Kathrine said, not knowing how to respond.

"Hey," Danny, Genni's dad, turned toward Zach. "Zach," he nodded.

"How are you?" Kathrine asked.

Beep. The hospital machines buzzed in the background. He didn't answer her question.

"How is Evelyn?" he asked.

Zach shot his awkward eyes at Kathrine.

"She's okay," she said with a smile. "She's going to make it."

"Well, isn't she lucky…"

42

"She is too much of a mess," Deputy Evans pointed at Natalie through the one-way mirror into the interrogation room. Natalie sat at the metal table; the one bright light above her bounced off the table and into her swollen eyes. The red rings around her eyes were daunting; she was so tired. So weak.

"She's not RED," Sheriff Mullins leaned away from the glass. "But we have to handle the gun situation."

"RED will feed off this. You know that, right?" she asked the sheriff.

"Sadly, I know," he positioned his heavy belt back into its place on his hip and opened the heavy door.

At the table, he reached forward to pat Natalie on the shoulder. She didn't move.

"How did you get the gun, Natalie? It's going to be okay."

She pulled her hands from her lap and covered her face. She wanted to tell the truth; she really did. But she didn't want to get Robert in trouble. What would happen to him? She loved her mom and step-dad. *He is okay, and he still loves you* she had to reassure herself.

She dropped her hands onto the table. Her tear-covered eyes looked up and met Sheriff Mullins'. Her chapped lips popped open for the first time in hours. "My step-dad gave it to me."

"Robert?" he asked.

"Yes." Her head dropped back to look at the table.

He stood up from the reflective table and grabbed the large door handle. "Thank you, Natalie." She didn't look up.

"So he gave it to her for what? Protection?" Deputy Evans asked from the other side of the glass as Sheriff Mullins emerged.

"Yeah... and I don't blame him."

"Where to next?"

"She'll need to go to a mental institution. She's not ready for the world," he rubbed his chin.

"Is anyone?" Deputy Evans walked away.

"Wait," the sheriff rose his hand.

"Yeah?" she turned back around.

He turned his head from the window to his deputy, "Sweep the Robert thing under the rug. Okay?"

Deputy Evans nodded, spun on her heels and continued walking away.

The smell of cigarettes seeped from the indention in the outside wall of the high school. The "too-cool-for-school" kids were passing a cigarette, not because they liked it, but it was the cool thing to do.

Derrick walked by and smelt the nicotine and chemicals from the lit end of the cigarette. He stopped. *Not again. No thanks*, he thought.

"Hey, Derrick!" the boy in the navy-blue hat stuck out the cigarette into the light from the shadowed corner.

"No, thanks," he walked away.

"What's gotten into him?" they whispered to each other.

"Probably the whole RED thing," the boy in the deep-green shirt took the cigarette.

"Give me that or I'll kill you," he joked.

"Ooohhh, go get your red hoodie," they laughed.

Derrick couldn't hear them, nor did he want to. He just kept walking to the almost empty parking lot. He fumbled through his pocket looking for his cold keys. When he looked up, he noticed a truck sitting just a few spaces from his... but it was strange.

Usually, a pretty girl in a blue Mustang parked there. This was a white truck... and the closer he got, Derrick noticed the man in the driver's seat was staring at him. Watching him come closer to his car.

As Derrick made it to his car, he finally realized who was sitting in the driver's seat.

"Oh, that's just Genni's dad, Danny... what is he doing here?" he whispered to himself.

43

Derrick turned the keys in his ignition and started his car. *Brumm*. The engine rattled.

The exhaust behind the car steamed up into the cold air.

Danny copied him and started his truck just seconds after Derrick. *Brumm*.

Derrick looked over at Danny and nodded. It was terribly awkward, but it's all he knew to do. He looked back at the parking lot in front of him and pulled toward the exit, rolling over the white lines on the pavement. Derrick's eyes were glued to his rearview mirror, watching Danny's white, rusty truck. He turned the heat higher; if it wasn't already cold enough, the anxiety was making it colder. And just like magic, right on cue, Danny's truck started to pull to the exit behind Derrick.

The red light turned green. "Oh," he said. He pulled out and stayed in the right lane, hoping Danny wouldn't follow behind. He kept going, keeping the speed low... and so did

Danny. Derrick kept watching the rearview mirror more than the road.

"This is weird! What are you doing, man?" Derrick said to himself. "Oh. No... surely not..." He wanted to convince himself that Danny wasn't waiting on him in the parking lot. That he wasn't following him.

But, Derrick's photo was in Danny's cabin. Hanging beside all his friends, the pictures were like a wall of fame. A hanging collection of faces that meant something. But these friends were here and alive... and Genni wasn't.

Derrick pulled into a hardware store, praying that Danny would keep going. But like seeing a monster crawl in a scary movie... the rusting truck pulled in just seconds after.

"This isn't cool, man," Derrick said. His eyes shot to the gas station that shared the parking lot. The sunset meant one thing to Derrick: those lights above the pump were about to come on. Derrick pulled forward and parked at the pump under the flickering light, even though his tank was full of gas.

It was a waiting game. Like cat and mouse. Who's moving first? The cat? Or the mouse? Danny knew Derrick was onto him. He picked up the gun from the passenger seat and moved it into the glovebox. "Not today," Danny said.

Derrick, lucky enough, watched Danny pull out of the gas station and head the opposite direction... but that wasn't enough for Derrick. He knew Danny was up to something, but he had to know more.

He put the car into drive and turned the cat into the mouse.

44

Left. Right. Down the street. Left. Right, again. Derrick followed Danny down every street throughout the town. He wasn't trying to lose Derrick; Danny obviously had a destination. But Derrick made sure to keep his distance and did a better job than Danny did. Danny had no idea he was being followed.

Danny's thumbs bounced off the worn steering wheel over and over again. He kept sliding his lip into his mouth and was biting a little too hard. The chapped lips were on the verge of bleeding, but he wouldn't even notice the taste of iron. His nails were down to almost nothing. His eyes went from darting around in every direction to simply staring at the road. His foot was getting heavier and heavier on the pedal until he zoned back into reality.

Finally, he saw where he was going. He perched up from his slump and looked around the parking lot. He made it to his destination… and the person he was meeting was here, too.

Derrick slowed down and let Danny pull into his destination a few minutes sooner.

"I can't go over there," he said. He turned to the left and pulled into the old recycling center. The streets weren't even slightly busy. He got out of his car and locked the doors. He hit the lock button again just in case. He pulled his gray gloves from his warm pocket and slipped them onto his hands. "Why is he going to the cemetery?" he asked out loud.

The gravel under his feet crackled as his boots shifted down the road. He reached the cracked corner of the building next to the cemetery. "SAWMILL" was plastered on the side. He leaned down and pivoted so that he could watch Danny and his friend.

Danny stood from the other side of his truck and walked closer to the cemetery. As he passed the only other car in the parking lot, he slammed his palm down on the hood. Anger? Or did he know the driver?

The driver's door of the car creaked open. Danny walked around to the driver's door and stood in the way of seeing the identity. The denim button-up was flapping in the wind. His white undershirt was dirty, and his boots still had mud around the bottom.

"They know each other, but why the cemetery?" Derrick whispered. "What are they meeting for?"

Finally, Danny moved to the left and hands emerged from the darkness to grab the upper door frame of the car. A man pulled forward and leaned out of the car.

The man seemed familiar... Derrick had seen him before. Who is that? he thought.

"Oh!" Derrick gasped. "That's the man from the cemetery. His son Steven was killed years ago..." Derrick pulled out his phone and stared at the screen. He didn't need it for anything, but it helped him think. The screen turned black.

"Genni... Genni Fisher," Derrick slid his phone back into his pocket. "Danny is meeting with... his dad?" Derrick looked closer.

"Danny didn't *just* lose his daughter... but his brother, Steven, was murdered years ago, too..." he whispered.

What are you doing Danny? he thought.

45

"This is crazy… Danny's brother was killed years ago and then Genni?" Derrick's shaking hands fumbled as he tried to pull his phone from his pocket. He bit down on the fuzzy yarn of his gloves and slid them off. He kept them between his teeth as he typed.

Man, I'm coming over. I have to tell you something crazy. Are you home? He texted Zach.

He acted normal as he moved from the corner of the building back to his car. The butterflies and energy made him want to run, but he couldn't make a scene. If he did that, Danny and his dad would notice him in the distance. He kept his cool and kept his pace. His breathing was heavy, but he was getting it to slow down. He put his gloves back on his hands.

He looked over his left shoulder back toward the cemetery. Gone. He couldn't see them anymore. Now he could go.

He took off running, kicking gravel up with every long stride. He grabbed his keys and had them ready as soon as he got to his car. He had to tell Zach. Everyone had to know that Danny was more involved than they thought.

He slammed the heat as high as it could go. He rubbed his hands together.

"Oh, my gosh..." he said.

He threw his gloves off again and into the passenger seat. He pulled out his phone and checked to see if Zach had texted back yet. He hadn't.

"Ugh, Zach. Come'on, man." He threw his phone into the cupholder and pulled away towards his house.

"I like what you're wearing today," Zach smiled at Kathrine in his living room.

"Thank you," she blushed.

"Why do you always say it like that?" he asked with a smile.

"Like what?" she grinned.

"The way your voice gets softer," he moved closer to her on the couch. "Do I make you nervous?"

She grinned but tried to hide it. "Yeah, you do, Zach." She brushed her hair behind her ear. "But it's just butterflies."

"Good," he said looking at her lips.

Bing. Zach's phone on the coffee table buzzed with Derrick's name.

"Derrick messaged you," she pointed at the table.

"Who cares?" he didn't take his eyes off Kathrine.

"What if it's important?" she asked.

"It's not."

Kathrine did what she does best: put up her walls. She rose her hand and put it on his chest. She applied pressure from the tips of her fingers. Not enough to cause conflict, but enough to send the message that he was too into the moment. She didn't like her walls being messed with like this.

"Oh. Sorry," his voice was sterner as he looked away.

"No, *I'm* sorry. You're not really doing anything wrong. I'm just not there yet."

She didn't mean to offend him, but that's how he took it.

"It's okay," he lied.

His phone buzzed again. *Let me know when you're home,* Derrick sent him.

Derrick changed destinations and went home to his lonely house. Nobody else was home... the only sounds in the house were from the forgotten television. The news was on, but nobody was watching. He slumped down on his bed and slid his phone onto the end table.

"Ugh," he groaned. "I just want my friends back."

It was just a message without a response. He was probably busy and wasn't doing this on purpose. Zach wasn't *really* trying to ditch Derrick... but it was easy to think that.

Maybe he is. Maybe he is actually done with me just like everyone else, he thought. *I don't deserve their forgiveness anyway...*

Then, his phone buzzed on the table. He was hoping to see Zach's name, but it wasn't. It was Evelyn.

Hey, I'm home from the hospital and doing fine. I wanted to get coffee with you if you wanted.

He smiled at his phone.

Sure. Be at the coffee shop in ten?

Yeah!

I have crazy news to tell you, Eve.

46

"Genni's dad—" Derrick started.

"Danny," Evelyn finished. The smell of coffee was strong. The clinking of glasses ringed in the coffee shop. It wasn't busy, but there were a few scattered friend groups under the fancy decorations. Evelyn and Derrick were sitting on the lime green couch in the corner.

"Yeah, Danny. He didn't *just* lose Genni."

Evelyn's eyebrows rose. "Oh, no."

"I know. Danny lost his daughter *and* his brother."

"His brother? When?"

"Years ago… it was a murder or something," Derrick took his baseball cap off and sat it on the end table next to his coffee.

"That's RED…" Evelyn's eyes scanned the floor as she tried to piece things together. "Danny is RED."

"I think so…"

"But, wait. That doesn't make sense. He wouldn't kill his own daughter…"

"Maybe he went crazy? Danny is involved *somehow*," Derrick was trying his best to put everything together.

"What do we do?" she asked.

"I don't know. An anonymous tip to the sheriff?" Derrick suggested.

"Yeah, you can't bop in there and tell them anything. They hate you," she chuckled.

Derrick rolled his eyes and took a sip of his steaming coffee. "On another note, how are you feeling? You look good."

"Thank you! I feel it," she smiled and placed a hand on her gunshot wound. "I'm healing, and I don't think it'll be a problem. I mean yeah, it hurts, but that's what pain pills are for. I'm good," she smiled again.

"Have you heard from Zach?" Derrick changed the subject.

"Yeah, of course. I live with him."

"Well, I didn't know. He's obsessed with Kathrine. I don't know who he talks to." Derrick's voice was getting snippy.

"He's ignoring you?"

"Yeah, but it's okay. It's whatever," he took another sip of his coffee. "I mean, I don't think he means to, I just want him to be the same with me. I apologized to him and he seemed fine. Now that he has Kathrine it's like I don't matter anymore."

"That's not true, Derrick."

"It's okay. I'm cool with it…"

"Well, you don't seem like it…"

"What are we going to do about Danny?" he changed the subject again.

"It's getting late, Zach," Kathrine said in Zach's car. The windows were getting foggy and the heat in the car was doing the best it could. She kept reaching over from the passenger seat and turning on the windshield wipers so she could see through the foggy glass.

"I know, but I don't really care," Zach kept looking at her lips.

"Oh, my gosh. Why don't you just write some poetry already," Kathrine popped her knuckles.

"What do you mean?" he laughed.

"You're just sweet, Zach." She turned from looking out the windshield to him. She flashed her pretty white teeth with a grin. She looked down from Zach's eyes to his lips.

She leaned forward slowly, and he followed her lead. He closed his eyes and planted his lips on hers. Like a magnet, their chemistry was finally getting on the same field. The poles were spinning in unison.

He reached his hand down and unclipped his seatbelt. He reached forward and put his hand behind her smooth hair. He pulled her closer and made the butterflies in her stomach hit another level.

Zach's beard was tickling her face as he kissed her, and she liked it. She reached for his shoulders, not knowing what to do. She had never felt this nervous, or this warm. She wanted to keep this moment forever, so she opened her eyes.

When she did, she saw more than just Zach. The windshield was fogging back up, but it wasn't fogged enough to hide the view. Through the misty glass was a red figure, just out of the shining of the headlights.

47

"Stop! Zach!" Kathrine yelled as she pulled away from him.

Zach leaned back and threw his hands up. "What, Kathrine? I'm sorry! I didn't mean—"

"No! There he is!" Kathrine pointed through the foggy windshield to the red figure in the distance.

"Who? RED?" he leaned forward in his seat and put the car in reverse.

Kathrine reached down and slammed the heat as high as it would go. She spun the nozzle to defrost the windshield.

"We're getting out of here," Zach reached across and propped his arm over the back of Kathrine's seat. He looked backward and slammed on the gas. They pulled to the left as he repositioned the car to get back on the nearest road.

Kathrine spun back and tried to see what it was that faded away into the darkness as they drove away. Was it RED? Or was it paranoia?

"We're safe," Zach said.

"Should we call the police?" she said.

"Are you sure it was RED?"

"… I don't know," she turned back around and sunk into the seat.

Zach reached over and grabbed her hand. Their fingers interlocked as they went out into the night.

Derrick was in his room once again. Alone.

He kept walking back and forth from corner to corner. His room was usually a mess, but this time there wasn't anything to dodge as he walked the room. No clothes to step on, no books to step over. Even the chair in the corner was empty. Everything was put away. He had his room clean, except for his desk. The laptop was open to a google search. Printed papers from the school library were scattered on the desk. Lines were drawn from sheet to sheet and Genni's family tree was drawn on a sheet of notebook paper.

He stopped pacing and turned to his bed. He lifted his pillow from the smooth sheets and fluffed it one more time. He put it down and sat on the edge facing his desk.

Danny... Danny. Danny Fisher. He couldn't get his name out of his head.

He leaned over and pulled his phone from the end table. No notifications.

Zach, I am trying to piece it together man. This RED stuff has something to do with family.

The blue bubble on his screen had the word 'Delivered' under it for a few minutes. He was hoping Zach would respond quickly and start the conversation like he used to. Five minutes later, Zach started typing.

Then, he set the phone down.

Fifteen minutes later, Zach finally sent a message back to Derrick.

Oh, cool

Derrick looked at his phone with his eyebrows scrunched together. He didn't want to roll his eyes, but he had to.

I've been doing a lot of research. Genni's dad, Danny, lost his brother years ago. It was a murder.

Oh wow

This has something to do with family.

No response.

I really want my friends to be safe. I'm having trouble sleeping. Derrick told him the truth.

That sucks. Sorry man!

Derrick didn't know how to respond to that. He didn't want to waste his time... or Zach's. He wanted his best friend back but didn't want to put up with the embarrassment of rejection. Derrick felt that feeling in his throat. The feeling he was taught to hold back.

He locked his phone and sat it back on the nightstand. He moved onto the bed and rolled over. He wasn't going to be able to sleep... but he didn't want to be awake.

48

"When can I leave?" Natalie leaned against the front desk. Her labeled bracelet pressed against her wrist 24/7 and was making it itch. The barcode and letters gave her an identity to the doctors, but she wanted to rip it off.

"You guys have to see that I'm not crazy." She pulled her hair to the side and made sure to keep her cool. She didn't want to be locked here any longer. "I messed up, and it was an accident."

"Ma'am, we are doing everything we can."

The smell in this wing of the mental institution was sterile, like a bomb of high-class Germ-X exploded on the walls, which was strange to Natalie. It smelt and looked like a hospital, but she didn't think she was sick.

"Baby..." Pam, Natalie's mother, said from the door to the youth wing.

"Mom!" Natalie felt it like a tidal wave. She hadn't seen her mother in just a few days, but it felt like years. She ran to her mom's arms and let the tears rush down. They were dripping down onto her mom's shoulder, and it wasn't the first time the pink sweater soaked up her tears.

"I love you. I love you. I love you," she kept saying. She hadn't said it enough, and she needed to let it all out.

"I love you, too, honey. It's going to be okay. I'm taking you home today." Pam wasn't playing games. She came here for her daughter, and she demanded she was going home with her.

"Ma'am, you'll need to sign in here," the lady at the front desk picked up a clipboard and sat it on the counter.

Pam moved closer to the desk and leaned over. "I'm not signing anything besides release waivers."

"She'll need to be discharged by the doctor," the lady with stringy red hair was moving her papers into files. Natalie's was next.

"Where's the doctor at?"

"She should be coming in here in about twenty minutes, ma'am."

194

"Great. I'll be here," Pam grabbed her purse and Natalie's hand.

Back in Fayetteville, the cemetery had its usual visitors. Danny accidentally left his headlights on in the gravel parking lot. He sat beside his brother's tombstone. Then, he would walk to his daughter's.

He kneeled down into the cold mud. The weather was making his fingers hard to move. They couldn't curl up the way they normally would, but he was still able to rub the grass on her grave like it was Genni herself... but it wasn't. It was just grass. Under the ground was a platinum container with her body.

It wasn't enough, so he thought he needed to do more. He rubbed his scruffy beard that was getting too long. He wasn't wearing his wedding band, but he kept trying to spin it around his ring finger the way he used to before he took it off.

"Everything that's going to happen is for you, Genni. I have to do this... for you," he whispered.

If Genni could have heard him, she would have toned him down. She would have told him "no."

Genni wasn't here anymore... but someone was...

Across the cemetery at the far building—where Derrick was watching him before—was someone in a red hoodie.

49

Danny parked his car at his house. He stepped toward the house but turned to the left. He passed the shutter-covered windows and stepped over the dead leaves. The crunching would tell everyone where he was going.

He thought he was alone... but there was someone behind him. Keeping their distance and their red hoodie on, they had been to this house before. They watched Danny. He *had* to go. He couldn't keep digging into this.

Danny made his way into the woods and kept going. He passed over the dry creek with mud sticking to the bottom of his boots. RED was following behind, pivoting behind trees to make sure he couldn't turn and see them. It was like a ghost in the distance watching Danny, making sure every move was accounted for. Danny wasn't getting away.

Where are you going, Danny, RED thought. Their breath was moving up in the cold air. Even though RED had a backpack full of weapons and tools to take Danny out, they were still scared. Their heart was beating. Faster. Faster.

Almost out of their chest. Their breathing was heavy, but they were getting better at keeping it quiet.

"There," RED whispered. Their eyes followed Danny as he moved into the tiny cabin.

Danny pulled his blanket off the table to reveal all of his papers and sat his gun on the table. The red yarn connecting dots. Pictures of all of Genni's friends. Danny's own personal detective board was connecting what he could find. He wasn't getting too close to RED's identity, but little did he know... RED was already physically close.

"Who are you," Danny leaned into his desk. "I'm going to find you."

He felt it. Boiling. Heart beating. Tingling fingertips. He grabbed the gun from the table and sat in the corner in the chair. He leaned back and moved his finger closer to the trigger. He pointed it at the wall with Genni's friend's pictures.

Pop.

Danny looked over at the window. He heard something. Something hit the window.

"Was that a rock?" he said out loud.

198

Then, in the distance behind a tree, he saw it. That red hoodie. RED was standing right there. He tightened his grip on the gun and slung the door open. The cold hit him in the face, but he didn't notice. He bolted down the wooden path and moved over to the left. He kicked up leaves and crunched over sticks. It was loud and obvious, but he didn't care. He was running as fast as he could.

"You're mine!" he yelled. He stopped and pulled his gun out. He pointed it at the hoodie.

"Come out. Let me see you."

Nothing. The shoulder was sticking out from behind the tree.

"Say something! Who are you!?" he yelled.

It was so silent the leaves moving from the wind could be heard.

"Can't say a word, can you?" Danny pivoted around the tree and pulled the trigger. The bullet hit the red hoodie.

Poof.

The pillow inside the red hoodie nailed to the tree barely moved after the bullet went through the fabric.

"No!" the veins in his throat could be seen as he yelled.

He lunged forward after noticing a piece of paper around the nail. The red marker bled through the notebook paper.

"NOT THAT EASY"

He turned back around, looking at the cabin. He pulled the gun up, again. Ready to shoot.

"I've got you now," he said with what breath he could as he ran back to the cabin.

He stood just off the porch and looked into the open front door. He lifted the gun. "Go ahead. Destroy all my evidence. Destroy my work. It doesn't matter because you're dead."

Danny squeezed the trigger three times.

BAM. BAM. BAM.

He bolted forward and slung open the door. He thought he would see splattered blood on the back wall of the tiny cabin. He thought RED was inside.

Nothing.

Danny slung his head around, looking through the windows. He was so angry that he didn't notice the clear liquid running over the window. He had stepped over it in the doorway, too.

"No, I've got *you*," RED yelled from outside the cabin.

RED ran the match over the box and sparked the end with a small flame. RED slung their arm forward and let go of the match.

The liquid at the doorframe, the gasoline, went up first. Then, the flames quickly moved over to the windows. Every exit to the tiny cabin was lit. Burning the gasoline... then the wood of the cabin.

RED pivoted away and let the cabin turn from wood to ash... with Danny inside.

50

Evelyn tapped her purple pen on the ugly desk over and over. She stared at the whiteboard with assignments written in the corner of the board.

PAPER DUE FRIDAY

She didn't care. It was Wednesday, and she hadn't even started on that stupid paper. Maybe she'll crank it out tonight, or maybe even Thursday night. It was like school was the last thing on her mind. She didn't even focus in class anymore. She used to make good grades, but now she didn't even know what her grade was in this class—or any other.

The doorway had students walking through it from time to time. The class was starting soon, and everyone was making their way from the lunchroom. Every time someone walked in, Evelyn would turn and see who it was; then she would turn her head back to her desk within a second.

Then, someone walked in that held her attention. In fact, she almost gasped.

Natalie brushed her hair off her shoulder as she stepped into the classroom. She spun the necklace around her neck and let it dangle down onto her chest in the opening of her green jacket. She sat down in her desk, the closest one to the door.

Evelyn sat down her purple pen and got up from her desk. She placed her hand over her wound that Natalie herself had given her. She walked up the row of desks and walked over to Natalie's.

"You're back," Evelyn smiled.

"I figured you wouldn't be interested," Natalie pointed at Evelyn's side where Natalie had shot her.

"No! I would love to talk sometime! I'm not mad at you. I'm okay," she extended her knees and hopped off the ground. "See?"

"I feel so bad, Evelyn," Natalie rubbed her forehead.

"For not telling anyone you were back? Or shooting me?" Evelyn laughed.

Natalie cracked a smile and shrugged her shoulders. "I guess both," she said with a playful eye roll.

Then, a boy emerged from the doorway and bumped shoulders with Evelyn. He didn't turn or acknowledge her; he just kept walking to his back-corner desk.

"Umm," Natalie said.

Evelyn turned around with her hands out. She thought it was so rude that he would bump into her and not say anything like that. Then, the boy turned down his row of desks and she saw his face.

His cheeks were flushed, and his eyes were swollen red. His nose was running but not from allergies. He tried to turn his face to hide the wet streak down his cheeks. He didn't want his class to see that he had been crying, and he sure didn't want anyone to ask him about it. That would only turn the waterworks on even more.

"Oh, poor guy," Evelyn whispered.

"What's wrong?" Natalie asked.

The girl sitting behind Natalie looked up from her phone. "His parents are getting a divorce."

Natalie turned around and Evelyn leaned in.

"*Adam Stone's* parents are getting a divorce?!" Natalie whispered.

"Yep. That's what I heard," she said.

"Welcome to the club... poor guy," Evelyn said.

"You should go talk to him," Natalie told her.

"I will after class." Evelyn turned back for her desk.

RIIING.

"That's the bell," the teacher stood from her desk at the head of the room.

51

The bell rang, and the teacher was still pumping out whatever English lesson they were learning that day. But when the bell rang, *the bell rang*. It didn't matter if the teacher was in the middle of the most important thing in the world... *class was dismissed.*

"Hey," Evelyn reached forward and grabbed Adam Stone's arm as he walked in front of the classroom. His felt jacket was soft on Evelyn's fingers. The jacket seemed like it cost more than a hundred dollars.

"What?" Adam turned around. He stopped in his tracks and was willing to look at Evelyn. Before class started, he wasn't really able to hold back his emotions, and everything was being let out. Now, his eyes had gone back to looking normal, and his cheeks weren't flushed red anymore.

"I'd like to talk with you... if that's okay," Evelyn asked, still holding on to his arm.

"About what?" Adam didn't tug his arm away from her.

206

"I just want to make sure you're okay… I think we can relate," Evelyn let go of his arm. "It's important to talk about stuff."

"I guess so…" Adam looked around the room as the other last student walked passed them and out the door. "Where at?" he asked.

"We can go anywhere really. How does Ken's sound? I love their burgers," she smiled.

"I've never been to Ken's."

"Well, let's go!" Evelyn smiled.

Derrick was walking into the grocery store across the road from the school. The blue welcome sign shined above his head as the automatic doors opened in front of him. Through the doors, he looked to his left at the shopping carts. To his right, Zach and Kathrine were walking—hand in hand—with a few white plastic bag around their wrists.

Derrick rose his hand to wave; a smile ran across his face. Zach and Kathrine didn't break eye contact with each other. They giggled and looked only at each other as people passed them. They were walking straight for Derrick at the door, but they couldn't even look up at him.

As they got closer, Derrick dropped his hand back to his side and let his smile turn into something else. His eyes hit the floor and his shoulder sunk lower. As they made it to the door, Derrick looked up one last time to see if they would notice him.

Zach grabbed Kathrine's bag and turned his shoulders toward the door. They walked out, and Derrick nodded his head. He knew it was getting worse. He knew his friendship with Zach was crumbling when he needed it most.

Outside in the car, Zach opened Kathrine's door and let her take a seat. He tossed the plastic bags into the back seat where he would probably forget them. He got into the driver seat and started the engine. As he looked back and put the car in reverse, he remembered what he was forgetting to tell Kathrine.

"Oh yeah! I'd been meaning to tell you about last night," Zach said.

"What was last night?" Kathrine asked with her head deep into her phone.

"It's about Evelyn," Zach's tone changed. He was a little more serious.

Kathrine locked her phone and dropped it to her lap. "What is it?"

"I heard her last night in her room... She seemed to be doing really well about being shot and everything. She always seems to be in a good mood and seeing the best in things, right?"

"Yeah! I don't know how she does it," Kathrine put her elbow on the console between them and leaned her head on her hand.

"I think it's all an act... she was crying really hard in her room last night."

"Did you talk to her?"

"I tried... she wouldn't let me. I knocked on the door and asked to come in. She chirped up and shooed me away. She was trying to act like herself, but I know deep down, she's hurting."

"Try to talk to her again today," Kathrine suggested.

"I will if I can," Zach said.

52

The photographer let the shutter click in their camera as the flash went off. Sheriff Mullins stood behind them next to Deputy Evans. The red hoodie nailed to the tree was sagging lower than when Danny shot it.

Surrounding them was yellow police tape wrapped around and between the trees. The wind was making it flap in the air. Other cops were walking around in the crime scene perimeter. The blue lights were flashing in the distance.

"They left a note," Sheriff Mullins crossed his arms.

"Not that easy," Deputy Evans repeated the note. "Was this for us? Or for whoever is in that cabin?"

Deputy Evans walked away from the tree and toward the burned cabin. "They didn't just kill someone out here... they were up to something."

Sheriff Mullins followed at Deputy Evans' side. "With Genni and Jasper, it was a crowbar. With the Thompson boy, it was a gun." He leaned down and grabbed a small log and tossed it from their path. The orange leaves were crunching beneath their feet. "If this was RED that burned this cabin and killed the man inside, why did he do it like this?"

"RED didn't just kill them... they took out his cabin, too. Something was in this cabin."

Sheriff Mullins leaned back in his leather chair at his desk. His arms were still crossed. "If you had a daughter that was killed and the murderer couldn't be caught, what would you do?"

"I'd go out and kill the psycho that did it," Deputy Evans said. "I wouldn't sleep until he was dead."

Mullins uncrossed his arms and reached out. He unraveled his hand and pointed at the photo of the steaming cabin. "He was after RED."

"And somehow RED caught onto it?"

"He got too close..." he crossed his arms again.

They didn't really need the photo on the desk. The image was scorched into their brains. They could remember the smell of the burnt wood, the burnt flesh.

212

The cold air made the warm logs steam more than usual. The logs of the cabin were crispy, and the black ashes looked like a pile of charcoal. Under the ashes were what was left of Danny and all his evidence and accusations. RED took it all out with a toss of a match: the evidence, the puzzle pieces, and Danny himself.

"What did Danny do that was so special? RED knows we're out for him, and he hasn't killed us—not yet anyway—but what about Danny made RED want to kill him?" Evans looked down at her badge, then met eyes with Mullins.

Sheriff Mullins picked up his phone and called someone in the next room. "I want Danny's everything. I want his texts, his emails, his google searches, I want to know what he had for breakfast last week. I want everything on him… make it happen."

Deputy Evans waited for Mullins to hang up the phone." And how did RED figure out that Danny was onto him?"

"Stalking? Maybe RED was watching him. He was after Genni at some point. Maybe it's about the Fisher family."

"And what about that?" Deputy Evans pointed to the crowbar in the large plastic bag on the corner of the desk. Red spray paint was covering it. It was still a little sticky and was sticking to the insides of the bag.

"His trademark. He wanted to make sure we knew it was him."

"I know. I mean what are we going to do about that? RED has these trademarks now. It's like he's a mythical creature or something. Red hoodies and crowbars everywhere taking people out."

Sheriff Mullins pulled his hat lower over his face. "I'm about tired of RED killing people in my town. We're finding this bastard, and we're finding him fast." He tightened his fist around the arm of his chair. "It's one of those kids in Derrick's squad. They've been under our nose and we just play their games. *It's over.* We're cracking down."

Deputy Evans grabbed the corner of the bag with the red crowbar and walked out of his office.

Sheriff Mullins leaned forward in his empty office and spun his thumb around his index finger harsh enough to make it burn. "This isn't happening. Not in Fayetteville."

53

The corner of RED's bedroom was usually empty. An end table with a golden lamp seemed to be enough aesthetic to keep them happy. A charger strung from the outlet on the wall and over the end table to their bed. If it weren't for the lamp, the corner would be dark enough to hide something.

RED reached their hand down over and inside the lampshade. They grabbed the bulb and turned it until it unscrewed from the slot. They sat it back down to hold the bulb upright, but if someone turned on the lamp, it wouldn't light up.

It'll have to do, RED thought. These supplies have to go somewhere... RED's fingerprints were on the handles of the gas cans. They couldn't leave them out there with Danny and the burnt cabin.

RED pulled the end table out away from the wall. They sat the gas cans down in the dark corner and threw an old blanket over them. They reached down and tucked the blanket so that nothing could be seen. They moved the end table back in front of the covered gas cans, checked again to make sure the lamp wouldn't turn on, then leaned against their bed.

"Hey, Adam," Evelyn leaned in for a hug. The coffee shop was about half empty, but the smell of bitter coffee and flavorings were full.

"Hey, Eve, how are you doing?" Adam asked just to ask. He wasn't genuinely concerned with how she was doing; it's just what people asked to break the ice.

"I'm doing okay. My side where Natalie shot me is a little painful today," she chuckled. *Ice broken.* "Do you know Derrick?" she asked.

"Yeah, I've heard of him, but we're not really friends." Everyone's heard of Derrick at this point.

"I invited him to come and have coffee with us... if you don't mind?"

"No, that's fine!" Adam's family was pretty popular, so Adam was used to meeting new, random people all the time.

When Derrick showed up, he dropped his keys in the parking lot. He huffed as he shoved them back into his pocket. Rough day. He walked inside and met with Evelyn and Adam.

"Hey, it's Derrick," Derrick reached out to shake Adam's hand. Derrick's eyes seemed a little swollen. It's not something you'd notice, but once you did, you would know Derrick had been crying.

"I'm Adam!" he smiled. His handshake was firm.

They sat down together and let the small talk run the conversation for a while. Derrick had his coffee, Evelyn had her tea, and Adam was making new friends. It crossed Derrick's mind that he could ditch Zach and be friends with Adam. Maybe he wouldn't feel so lonely. After all, Adam hasn't been around. He didn't see Derrick at his worst.

"Yeah, my dad works so much for this town, and when he's not working he's out in the woods somewhere hunting. I don't get to see him as much as I'd like," Adam said.

Derrick's eyebrows rose on his face.

"My dad used to take me out hunting all the time. I don't hunt anymore... I never saw the joy in it," Evelyn told him.

"Me either," Adam said.

Something stuck with Derrick. *Adam's dad was "out in the woods somewhere hunting."*

Derrick slid back in his chair and pulled his phone from his pocket. He was back to searching the internet for clues. This time, he was searching someone new: Adam Stone.

54

Derrick threw himself back to his pillows. His bed was finally colder. It had been warm from him being in it all the time. He wasn't out and about the way he really wanted to be anymore. He was thankful for his meeting in the coffee shop with Adam and Evelyn, but he couldn't turn his mind off. He was obsessing over RED, almost as much as Danny was.

He didn't find anything on Adam online. The search only pulled up news articles and websites about his dad, one of Fayetteville's best doctors.

The other thing on his mind wasn't a crazy killer… it was how lonely he had felt lately. It was frustrating him. Like a bug he had accidentally swallowed, and he couldn't get it to stop. The butterflies flew around in his stomach and somehow it gave him anxiety. He was watching all of his closest friends move on… he didn't blame them, but it still sucked.

He needed a new start and was desperate for something new. He couldn't take any more of this going to his bed after school and worrying himself to death trying to find out who RED was. When was he coming back out? He thought of Genni. He thought of Jasper. He thought he would never get his mind back where he wanted it: in peace.

He picked up his phone and started a new group message. He rolled his eyes as he hit Zach and Kathrine's names, but he still wanted to see them. He added Evelyn, and even his ex-girlfriend, Natalie. Then, he added someone new: Adam.

Hey, guys. I feel like we haven't really gotten to get together! I want to hang out with you guys. Y'all should come over sometime soon. How does this weekend sound? Is everyone free?

Yeah! I'd love to! Evelyn replied.

Sounds good to me, Natalie sent.

Zach and Kathrine didn't respond for quite a while, and Derrick knew they wouldn't. Maybe they saw it and read the message… maybe they were somewhere in a parked car. Who knows.

My parents actually have a log cabin off the lake if you guys want to come to that instead! It'll be empty and away from everything in Fayetteville. My parents won't mind if I have you guys over. I've had people over there before! What do you think? Adam said.

Omg that sounds so fun. Let's do it. Evelyn sent back almost instantly.

Derrick looked over at his laptop on his desk where he had searched Adam Stone online again. He found nothing... but RED was smarter than that.

"Do I do it? Should I go?" Derrick whispered to himself. "RED could be anyone... is this a good idea?"

His mind went back to the other topic it sat on. He thought of how alone he would be sitting at home. He wanted to be safe, and he wouldn't ever give RED a chance to get him... but he wanted to live. He wanted to not just be alive. He had to have his friends. He had to get them back or there wasn't a point anymore. No more nights crying alone. No more wishing he had his best friend Zach back. He had to live, and hiding from RED kept him alive, but he wasn't living.

That sound so fun, man. Thanks! What time on Friday? Derrick sent.

55

Adam's boots were slushing in the mud in the backyard. He jiggled the keys to the shed in his left hand as he held gasoline cans in the other. The gas bounced and splashed around inside the container. He slid the key into the lock on the wooden door. He pulled the door open and put the gas cans away where they belonged.

"There we go," he smacked his hands together.

"Are you sure you want to do this?" Kathrine asked Zach from his passenger seat.

Zach turned off the highway and onto the long back road that took them to the lake house.

"Derrick's going to be there. I haven't seen him in a while," Zach said.

"Do you trust Adam?" Kathrine asked. "I'm okay with Derrick being mad at you if that means we don't have to deal with RED."

"I don't want to deal with RED either," he shrugged his shoulder. He thought that was obvious. "...but I'm sure we're safe," his voice was shaky.

"I don't know about this, babe." Kathrine rubbed her forehead.

"We won't stay long... how's that sound?" Zach was a little more enthusiastic about that.

"Thank you," she sighed with relief. She turned to him. "I want a code word."

The road was getting bumpier as the car bounced from pothole to pothole.

"Say your knee is hurting," Zach took his left hand off the wheel and rubbed his kneecap.

"Sounds good to me," Kathrine leaned back in the seat. "I'm nervous, Zach."

"Me too..." he whispered.

"Is Adam RED?" Kathrine said.

"If he is, he won't hurt you. I don't care what it takes to keep you safe. You're mine," he told her.

She could feel her heart rate rising. Anxiety? Love? She didn't know the exact word to place on it, but she liked this feeling. The warmness on the inside... she hadn't felt this way since Florida.

"He's not RED." Zach turned on the turn signal and pulled into the long driveway. As his headlights finally broke through the darkness and hit the lake house, there he was.

Adam leaned with his left hand on the front door for support as he yanked his muddy boots off his feet. He grabbed them by the opening and placed them on the first porch step. He leaned up and waved at the approaching car.

Pam held her daughter tight. She didn't want Natalie to go out to the lake house, but she knew she needed it. She was going to be okay. At least, that's what she kept telling herself.

"Natalie... I know Sheriff Mullins has the gun..." Pam let go of Natalie and grabbed her hand. "I need my baby to still be here in the morning." Pam walked out of the kitchen and into her and Robert's bedroom. She emerged from the green door frame with something for Natalie.

"I haven't asked Robert…" Pam opened her hands to another pistol. The gray barrel and wooden handle shined from the overhead kitchen lights.

"I messed up last time… I can't do it—" Natalie started.

"I don't care. If someone tries to hurt you—" Pam handed the gun to Natalie and wrapped her daughter's hands around it. "—you shoot."

"I love you, Mom." Natalie met eyes with her mom. Tears were starting to build up in Pam's eyes.

Natalie opened her bag and slid the gun inside.

Honk. Honk.

Natalie turned to the door. "Evelyn's here to get me."

"Don't shoot *her* again," Pam chuckled as she wiped her running nose from her emotions.

"Only if I have to," Natalie said. She zipped her bag and walked outside.

56

"I can't tell you enough how bad I feel," Natalie rose her hand and placed it under her left eye. She looked up, preparing for a tear to drop.

"Natalie, listen! It's okay. It really is," Evelyn reached forward and turned off the radio. "I'm a forgiving person. I feel like you have to forgive people in life. You don't need to beat yourself up over something that's over. It's in the past. I may have a pretty scar on my side to tell my kids one day," Evelyn giggled. "...but it's just a scar. It's just a story. The damage is done... but that's what scars are for. To show you the damage is *done*."

Natalie listened, and she knew. She knew Evelyn was right, and it made her cry a little more.

"Thank you, Eve." Natalie moved her bag from her lap to the floorboard. "I needed to hear that. I've been feeling down and upset about this whole thing. RED left a *big* scar... and he's still out there. It rocked my world... it really did."

"I don't think the scars from RED are fully here yet. We're still healing and trying to turn the wound into a scar, and that's okay."

Evelyn turned off the highway and onto the long backroad. Natalie let the silence linger in the car.

"I've felt like the wound for so long... I'm ready for it to just be a scar."

"Me too," Evelyn looked down at the potholes in the road. "Me too, Nat."

Natalie thought of her gun in her bag and pulled it from the floorboard and onto her lap. She felt like her guard was down, and strangely enough, she felt safe at the same time. At the lake house, she'd have the gun ready and close.

Evelyn parked the car behind Zach's in the dark driveway. She leaned over and grabbed Natalie's bag for her as she hopped out of the car. Natalie looked down and reached for it, but Evelyn bounced out of the car and shut the door too quickly. Natalie opened her door and slammed it shut. She spun around to Evelyn in front of the car. Evelyn smiled at Natalie.

"Thank you, but I've got it," Natalie reached forward.

Evelyn pulled away. "No, it's okay! I know you shot me and all but let me carry it for you!" She giggled.

"No, really, I've got it." Natalie's voice was sterner. She stepped forward again.

Evelyn tightened her grip on the bag. Her forehead wrinkled in confusion. She pulled back away from Natalie again. "Why are you being so weird, Nat?"

Natalie took a deep breath and lunged forward. She snapped her hand around the black bag, but Evelyn's grip didn't change. Natalie huffed.

She brought her other hand up, but this time she didn't go for her bag. She grabbed Evelyn's side where she shot her and squeezed. She let her nails dig a little harder into the scar.

"Give. Me. The. Bag."

57

Evelyn flinched and opened her hand. Natalie was standing so close to Evelyn that it landed on her feet. Natalie and Evelyn were about the same height, but with the determination and intimidation seeping from Natalie's eyes and into Evelyn's, Natalie seemed four feet taller.

Evelyn grabbed her side and gritted her teeth. "What's in the bag, Natalie?"

"My medicine. I just don't trust people anymore, okay?" Natalie snapped as she snatched her bag off the ground and onto her shoulder.

Natalie turned and walked to the front porch of the lake house. Evelyn stood at her car holding her wound where Natalie jabbed her fingers. She had a second thought:

Do I just turn around now? Do I just leave her here?

She pulled her phone from her pocket and texted Derrick.

Please get here soon. I miss you, and I don't know what has gotten into these people.

She didn't want to scare Derrick... but she wanted him here for her.

Natalie took a deep breath before opening the front door. She didn't knock. Evelyn did the same... took a deep breath, marched up the stairs, and walked through the open front door and shut it behind her.

"Hey, you two!" Adam said from the kitchen. He had a red and white apron on. He loved to cook for a pastime, but he was wearing this as a joke.

Natalie put on a fake smile and chirped. "Hey! How are you!? It looks like you're cooking us something great!"

"Oh, I am—" Adam and Natalie continued their conversation over the granite countertop. Natalie slid her shoes off and slung them into the shoe pile in the corner but didn't let go of her bag.

Kathrine and Zach sat at the other granite countertop holding hands. They sat on cushioned, wooden stools. They turned and started conversation with Evelyn.

"Hey, Eve!" Zach started.

230

"Hey," Evelyn wasn't trying to hold back as much as Natalie. She stood behind Natalie at an angle. Kathrine noticed the way Natalie and Evelyn were awkwardly not acknowledging each other, but she didn't say anything.

"Love the matching socks," Evelyn pointed to Zach and Kathrine's feet. Evelyn's phone buzzed in her pocket, but she didn't check it yet.

Adam's cooking was not only pretty, but it smelled delicious. His chicken was just right, and the smell was filling the entire kitchen.

"The food smells great, Adam." Kathrine let go of Zach's hand and leaned over the granite.

"Thank you! It's rotisserie."

"…and it smells good?" Kathrine asked.

"Well, I *am* an expert… I know how to season my chicken."

Kathrine looked over at Zach talking to Evelyn and thought of the real reason they're even here. "Where's Derrick?" she asked.

Zach perked up and turned toward the group. "Yeah, where is he?"

Evelyn pulled her phone from her pocket and saw Derrick's response.

I'm really sorry... I just don't think I can make it.

Evelyn moved over to the tan loveseat and dropped down on her phone.

I may need you for a ride

Yes, she drove and would explain that to him later... but she wanted him there, so she lied.

"Jasper would have loved to take your picture right now. I wish he was here..." Zach said.

It's true, Jasper would have taken so many pictures already... and the thing is, although it's just them standing around and having small talk, Jasper would have made this place look like a million bucks with his pictures. He was an expert. He was so talented, and he was so missed.

Everyone got silent, but not in a bad way. They all just took a moment to think about how different it would be if

Jasper was here. They miss him, but RED got him. Adam turned back to the chicken and had his back to the group.

Natalie tightened her grip on her bag and stepped down the hall into the bathroom. She locked the door behind her and slammed her bag on the sink counter. She grabbed the cold zipper and slid the blue bag open. She reached inside and felt the handle of her pistol. She slid it into the back of her jeans, just in case.

58

"Evelyn," Adam turned from the cooked food and grabbed five plates. "Do you think Derrick will be here soon?" he asked. "The food is done!"

Evelyn checked her phone again.

I'm sorry, Derrick's text said.

Evelyn rose her head and rolled her eyes. "I don't think he's going to make it."

"Bummer," Zach dropped his head.

"Well, we can't stop the feast!" Adam moved the plates to the table. "Grab a seat," he smiled.

Natalie stared into the mirror in the bathroom. She wasn't crying, but a week or two ago she would have been. Yeah, she missed Jasper, and she was under a lot of stress, but who wasn't? She pulled the back of her green shirt up and let it drop down over the gun sticking out of the back of her jeans.

She unlocked the door and dropped her bag by the shoe pile as she made her way to the table.

She sat at the end seat. Adam was at the other end facing her. To her right was Evelyn, and to her left was Kathrine. Zach was next to her.

"I fixed your plate," Evelyn smiled.

"Thank you, but I'm not that hungry," Natalie forced a smile at Evelyn.

Kathrine's fork screeched on her plate. Zach cringed and turned to her. "Oh, my gosh," he chuckled as he took another bite.

Adam looked up and made eye contact with Natalie. "Come on! You have to at least try a plate." He flashed his smile that got him any girl he wanted.

"No, I can't. It *does* look good though." She pushed the plate away from her.

"I didn't put all this work into making this food for you to push the plate away!" That could have been offensive, but Adam said it in a way that was playful.

Natalie turned the corners of her mouth up to at least give him something. It was technically a smile, but she didn't mean it.

"This food is so good," Zach said. He wasn't paying attention to their conversation at all.

Evelyn was staring at Adam then turned back to Natalie. She widened her eyes, confused. Natalie felt the awkward tension that she didn't mean to create. She pulled her phone from her front right pocket and set it on the table. She hit the home button. 1 bar of signal.

"So is Derrick coming or not, Eve?" Zach asked, then yawned. He covered his mouth so his mouth full of food didn't gross everyone out.

"I don't think he is coming at all."

"Huh," Zach finished his yawn. "I'm sorry." He blinked hard. "What did you say?"

Kathrine looked at Zach, worried. She looked at Adam… he was looking at Zach's plate. She took another bite and looked at Natalie, then Evelyn.

What is going on? Why is it so freaking awkward? Kathrine thought.

236

Zach drops his fork to the table. "My eyes are getting so heavy…"

Kathrine exhaled loud enough to hear it across the table. "Dang, I'm kinda sleepy, too." With the last bit of energy she had, she thought of the code word. "Zach, my knee is hurting."

Adam got up from the table and didn't push in his chair.

Evelyn leaned over to whisper to Natalie. "Um, what drugs did they take?" she laughed.

Zach's head slammed into his food. Mashed potatoes flung out into Adam's empty chair. Kathrine leaned for him and fell out of her chair and into the floor. Asleep. Out.

Natalie jumped and pushed her chair back. She looked around for Adam… nowhere.

Evelyn looked at Natalie. "AHHH!" she yelled.

Natalie reached for her gun and turned around to Adam standing behind her.

CLUNK. He hit her over the head, and she never saw it coming. She dropped to the floor.

"NOO! OH, MY GOD!" Evelyn yelled again.

59

Zach's eyes crept open. The room was lit by the warm overhead light. The walls were bare and painted an ugly tannish color. There were two windows facing the outside, and carpet covered the floor. A closet on one wall was left open, several red hoodies hung on the hangers. His wrists were behind his back and hurting from the pressure of the tight rope around them. His shoulder seemed on the edge of popping out of place. This room must have been a bedroom, but the furniture was recently moved. There were four indentions in the carpet from the legs of a bed that used to sit in here.

Zach looked straight across from him: Natalie, on the ground in the corner next to the left window. In the corner to his left, by the door, was Kathrine. In the other corner was Evelyn, next to the right window.

Natalie had blood dripping from her forehead at her hairline. She was moaning, trying to wake up. Zach looked at her feet. Her ankles were tied together by a rope that was woven through a heavy cinder block. He looked down at his feet... the same thing. All four of them had their hands tied behind their backs, and their feet bound together by a rope attached to a cinder block.

"RED," he whispered.

Natalie rose her head. "You mean *Adam*." She pulled her feet up to try and see if she could lift the cinderblock. She could, but not for long. Her skinny legs couldn't break free. She leaned her head back against the wall.

Throbbing at the pace of her heartbeat, her head was still warm and hurting from the hit in the dining room. She rubbed her fingers over her waistline from behind... nothing. Her gun was gone.

"I smell gasoline..." Zach whispered across the room.

"Me too," Natalie said. She tried to pull her wrists apart. Too tight.

Evelyn slung her head up from leaning on the wall. She frantically looked around the room. "NO!" she yelled again. She tugged at her feet and ankles to break free. She couldn't. There it was, running over her: panic.

"AHHH! HELP ME! HELP US! NO!!!"

"Evelyn! Shut up!" Zach whispered in an aggressive voice.

"NO NO NO!" she kept flaring her arms, trying to break free.

"Evelyn!" Natalie joined him.

"NOT US. NOT ME. WHY!?" she hollered.

"We need time… don't let him know we're awake!" he hissed at her.

"SHUT. UP." Natalie snapped.

Evelyn stopped and looked at Natalie. "What?!" she started crying. "You gonna shoot me again? Or just jab your fingers into my side?"

"What?" Zach looked at Natalie.

"This psycho really is trying to kill me. Are you working with him?" Evelyn snapped.

"No, Evelyn. Now is not the time for your bull crap. We need out of here. Stop it!"

"Not now, Evelyn. We have to get out of here."

"And just how are we going to do that? I can't even lift my feet," she started crying again.

Zach looked at Kathrine by the door... and his heart sunk. She's stuck in this too, and he can't save her. "No," he whispered. He dropped his head, then started pulling at his wrists again.

"How is she still asleep?!" Evelyn groaned.

"My phone is gone. Does anyone still have theirs?" Natalie looked at Evelyn.

"No," they said.

"What are we going to—" Evelyn stopped. She was interrupted by a sound that made them all freeze with adrenaline. Their hearts got faster. The hair on their arms stood up straight.

Clunk... Clunk... Clunk... Heavy footsteps were getting louder and louder from outside the room.

Click. The door handle started to wiggle.

60

The door crept open, letting more light slip in from the hallway. Then, *SLAM*. A hand hit the door and slung it open. The door swung back on the hinges and hit Kathrine on her right shin.

"Uhh," she groaned with her eyes still closed. She finally started to wake up. From the left of the doorframe, Adam emerged in the doorway. He stepped forward, letting his boots track mud onto the room's carpet.

"You son of a—" Natalie started.

"Son of a what?" Adam snapped at her. "Did you have a *gooood* nap, sweetheart? I thought you'd be dumb enough to eat my food... I guess not," he shrugged.

Adam pulled his phone from his pocket. He lined it up in front of Natalie and took a picture, letting the flash bounce off her face. Then, he turned to Evelyn.

"What are you doing?" she bent her knees and tried to kick. "Let me go!" she demanded.

Flash. Another picture.

"You… all along…" Zach shook his head. "Why did we come here?" he said.

Flash. Adam took another picture.

"Oh, she didn't want to wake up?" Adam grabbed the door and pushed it away, but it didn't close all the way. "*Waakkke uuuppp*, Kat." Adam was taunting them with his voice. He sounded like he was talking to kids. He reached down and slapped her across the face.

The pop was pretty loud.

"Don't you hurt her! You let us go right now! Let us go!" Zach was spazzing. His arms and legs were flaring as much as they could. Spit flung from his mouth. "Don't touch her!"

Kathrine jolted awake with a gasp.

"There we are," Adam smiled.

He leaned back and took her photo.

Flash.

"You're never going to get away with this," Natalie's voice was monotoned. She kept her head down, letting her hair hang over her face like a curtain. The blood from her forehead was starting to drip lower.

"I don't have to, Nat." Adam leaned his head over to one side as he stepped closer to her. "You see," Adam squatted before her. "Derrick has to get away with this."

"You idiot... he was in jail when you killed Jasper," Zach started to secretly tug at the rope behind his back. "Didn't think that one through, did you?"

"Oh, but I did," Adam stood up and turned to Zach. "The last one I kill will be Derrick's little helper... too bad you'll die in a scuffle right before the cops get here." Adam rose his hands and acted like a victim. "Help me! Oh, my God! Officers, I can't believe this happened. Oh, my God!" Adam repeated. "It was Derrick! And that one was helping him!" he smiled. "I walk away clean."

"Why?" Kathrine finally spoke up. Her voice cracked.

"Because some people don't care enough," Adam turned to Kathrine. "It's punishment. It's not anything you did... but this is only the beginning. Maybe now they'll care."

"Who?" Natalie asked, not really caring.

Adam turned to Natalie and stepped closer.

Now's my time. I have to do something, she thought.

Natalie kicked with her legs as hard as she could. She lunged forward, trying to bite at Adam's leg. He jumped back and reached behind him. He pulled Natalie's pistol from the back of his jeans. He lined up the gun with her head. "I wouldn't do that... *sweetheart*."

61

Evelyn broke down, her body shaking, she cried at the top of her lungs. Her chest started pumping in and out too quickly. She was hyperventilating.

Adam grinned and turned away from Natalie and over to Evelyn. He threw his hands down and made a crying sound. He frowned as he started to mock her. "Oh, no. Adam's gonna get me. RED finally got his way, *boo hoo hoo.*" He pointed the gun at Evelyn. "It's your time, Evelyn. It's finally time." He smiled.

He lunged forward and put the gun to her head. He grabbed her arm at the elbow crease and spun her around. The cinderblock weighed down her feet as he pulled her body to the center of the room.

"NOOOO!" she cried.

He put the gun back into the back of his jeans and pulled her body to the door.

"What are you doing to her?!" Kathrine yelled.

Adam grabbed her and tugged her out of the room. He huffed and pulled the gun back out from the back of his jeans and slammed the door shut.

"Oh, my God... What is he doing!?" Zach started.

"We can't do anything right here... we have to get out. We can't save her like this," Natalie said.

"Is that gasoline?" Kathrine asked.

"Yeah, it's over here on the lining of the window," Natalie answered. The windows went from the floor to the ceiling.

"Is he going to burn us down?" Kathrine asked, her voice getting more high pitched.

"Can you break the window with the cinder block?" Zach asked.

Natalie used her hands to pull herself away from the window. She spun on her butt and lifted her legs. With the adrenaline pumping through her veins, her heart was going faster than ever. She leaned back, picking up the cinder block and kicked as hard as she could at the window.

Crack. Klatishh. The glass shattered. The cold, winter air rushed in through the now open window.

"Oh, he definitely heard that." Zach started to lunge himself forward.

"Go! Let's go!" Kathrine started to wiggle her way to the window, too.

Natalie lifted her butt and slid her tied hands under it. She tried to pull them under, then over her feet and cinder block, but the cinder block was in the way... no matter how flexible she was.

"I can't get untangled," she groaned.

Kathrine lunged her way closer to Natalie. Zach looked at the closed door. "Hurry," he whispered.

Natalie pivoted herself so that her back was facing the broken window. "Kick me out the window," she demanded.

Kathrine didn't say a word. She picked up her legs and the cinder block as high as she could and kicked Natalie in the chest.

She flopped out of the window, through the broken glass, and landed on her back in the mud outside. The glass cut her back as she landed. "Uhhhh," she moaned.

She crawled and shuffled her way as far from the window as she could. Here comes Kathrine.

Thump. "Ouch," she flinched at the glass she landed on.

"Zach, hurry!" Natalie yelled.

Kathrine shuffled away from the window and looked up.

But it wasn't Zach.

Adam's head popped out the window. "Zach won't be joining you… and you can try, but you won't get very far!" Adam laughed and turned away from the window.

"ZAAACH!" Kathrine yelled.

"We have to get out of here!" Natalie yelled. "Come here!" she snapped.

Kathrine couldn't keep back her tears, but Natalie's adrenaline still had her heart going a mile a minute.

"Turn around; I can untie you," Natalie told her.

Kathrine spun around and leaned her hands back to Natalie's. With her hands still tied, Natalie pulled and tugged at Kathrine's rope to untie her hands.

"There, get mine," Natalie said.

Kathrine, still crying, turned around and started working on Natalie's wrists. Natalie looked over Kathrine's shoulder.

"...Hurry. Now!" Natalie screamed.

She could see him in the distance... making his way to them.

"What?! I've almost got it!" Kathrine cried.

"It's RED... he's coming!" Natalie screamed.

"There!" she cried, letting the rope around Natalie's hands fall to the mud.

"Shut up!" Adam yelled from inside the house.

Natalie's eyes shot open wide... RED was marching right for them... the crowbar swinging in his hands. Natalie and Kathrine's feet still tangled in the cinder block.

"That's not Adam," Natalie said, leaning away from RED.

62

"Go! Go! Go!" Natalie yelled. She and Kathrine both started pulling and tugging at their ropes as fast as they could.

"Is that Derrick?!" Kathrine screamed at Natalie.

"I don't know! Go!"

Natalie got her rope untied first. She jumped down at Kathrine's feet to help her.

"No, go. I've got this," Kathrine's voice changed.

"What about Evelyn? Zach?!" she asked.

"I don't know. Go!" Kathrine pointed to the woods.

Natalie stood up. She looked at RED getting closer. Now, he was running. She looked at the house and could hear Adam and Zach bickering back and forth inside the house. She looked behind her for the woods.

I have to... she thought.

"GO!" Kathrine yelled as she untied her feet and stood up. Kathrine didn't think twice and kicked up mud as she ran for the front door of the house.

Natalie spun on her heels and ran into the dark woods.

RED changed directions and chased after Kathrine. The distance was shorter, as RED was running straight to the front of the house, passing Evelyn's car, and Katherine was running to the porch. Kathrine's foot pressed against the first step... but she wasn't fast enough. RED was right behind her.

RED spun the crowbar so that the curved end wouldn't kill her. RED swung it like a baseball bat right at the back of Kathrine's head.

Clunk. Kathrine's body dropped to the steps like a heavy bag. Knocked out cold. RED looked up and could hear Adam in the living room of the house. Then, he looked back down at Kathrine. RED turned the crowbar around to the sharp end and lifted it up above his head. RED slung it down like a lumberjack cutting wood.

Splunk. Crack. The crowbar slammed into Kathrine's hip. The crowbar and the bone connected to create tension, and it wouldn't come back out easily. RED grabbed it and tried to pull Kathrine up the steps up of the porch. She was too heavy, and RED didn't want Kathrine to wake back up. He let go and jumped up the stairs and went inside to get Adam.

Adam emerged from the dark living room onto the front porch.

Adam stopped at her body. "Did you kill her? We wanted her alive..."

RED shook his head no. Adam shrugged his shoulders and grabbed onto the crowbar. He leaned down and pulled her up the steps and into the living room. Kathrine's blood was leaving a trail.

"That's a lot of blood," Adam looked at RED. RED bent down, grabbed the crowbar and twisted it out of Kathrine's hip.

Kathrine was knocked out on the floor with her blood creating a puddle. Zach was on the floor—about four feet away—still tied up with his hands behind him and a cinder block constricting his feet. RED and Adam stood in the center of the room.

"You let her get away!?" Adam snapped at RED. He kept Natalie's gun in his hand as he stepped closer to RED.

"Natalie can mess this all up. Why can't you just get that girl?" Adam turned his back to RED and stepped toward Kathrine. He pointed the gun at Kathrine. "Might as well end it... she's gonna bleed out."

Splunk. Adam's eyes shot open, and he shot a bullet at the floor. The gun fell from his hand and his knees started to give out. He grabbed his gushing neck; the crowbar was still sticking out of it. RED pulled the crowbar out of Adam's neck like pulling a knife out of jell-o. His blood shot out onto the floor between Kathrine and Zach like a fountain. He dropped to his knees and fell over.

RED bent down and grabbed the gun.

Kathrine gasped for air and grabbed her hip. "AHHH!" she yelled. She looked down, eyes wide and screaming. Her hip was throbbing, and blood was slipping out everywhere. She couldn't move her leg. It felt like a rock stuck on the inside, but it was just a gaping hole from the crowbar.

"Kathrine!" Zach yelled. He started crying. All he could do was watch Kathrine in her unbearable pain.

Kathrine looked up at Zach. "He's Derrick. Derrick is RED."

Zach looked at RED, still crying. "...that's not Derrick," he whispered, tears still falling.

RED reached up and grabbed the front of the hoodie with the hand not holding the gun. She pulled back her hoodie and let it drop down onto her shoulders. Evelyn looked down at Zach and Kathrine...

"No... I'm not Derrick," Evelyn said.

63

"What?!" Kathrine squeezed her hip tighter. "Evelyn... how could you do this to us!?" she screamed.

"You're dead, Ev. You're freaking dead." Zach lunged toward her, but the ropes and cinder blocks kept him from going anywhere.

Evelyn rose the gun to Zach. "No, if anyone is dead, it's you." She dropped the gun back down to her side. "But not yet..." she looked over to Adam's dead body. "I didn't really mean to kill you guys... it was a part of a bigger plan. This was punishment, and it just had to be this way."

"Punishment for what?" Kathrine cried.

"Not punishment to you... punishment to your parents." Evelyn looked over to Zach. "Our parents..."

"This doesn't make any sense," Zach gave up trying to break free.

"They just don't care. These parents care *so* much about everything *except* their kids," Evelyn shook her head. "Genni's

258

parents didn't care for her. They fought all the time... and she told me about it. She kept confiding in me—"

"Then, you killed her," Zach said.

"You picked me up that night... I got into your car!" Kathrine yelled at her.

"Yeah, Genni's body was in my trunk the whole time. While you were at the police station I dropped her body off in the river."

"Oh, my God," Kathrine looked down at her wound that was still bleeding too much.

"You killed Genni to get back at her parents?" Zach asked.

"Yes. To make her parents *care*." She lifted the gun and pointed it at Zach. "And our parents... they divorced and get married to each other and then run off to their honeymoon for a what? Two weeks? A year? They don't care! They don't care about us, Zach! Do you think they thought for a second how we felt? *No!*" she snarled.

"Jasper... how could you?" Kathrine asked.

"That was actually going to be his kill," Evelyn kicked Adam's body. "But, a car showed up and there were more people around than he thought so he let him live... that night."

"His parents seemed happy..." Zach started crying.

"I thought so too... until we had lunch one day. He told me that he was so bullied and everyone called him gay and a faggot. He said his parents didn't help. All they do is fight and they don't even notice him... So I had to make his parents finally notice him. Now, they do. They finally learned that they had a son."

"You're sick," Kathrine said.

"No, I'm not."

"And you framed Derrick..."

"Oh yeah, I wanted to plant it on someone with divorced parents. Maybe the cops would lock him up and see that maybe a divorce can make a kid go crazy."

"Apparently..." Kathrine said through her grinding teeth.

"Watch it, hun. You don't have much longer," Evelyn pointed at her bleeding hip with the gun. She turned to Zach.

"Derrick came and tried to fight you in *our* house. He had so much blinding anger that he left his car unlocked...idiot." She shook her head. "While you two were at it in the living room, I snuck out and slid the crowbar in his backseat. Made my job *so* easy." She flipped her hair off her shoulder. "Oh! And when we woke up in the room down the hall and I cried and yelled really loud... that was to let Adam know that you guys were finally waking up. He came in there, dragged me out of the room, and I put on my favorite hoodie."

"But what now? You killed your partner and Natalie got away."

"Now," she looked at her gun. "You have to die. You know too much... but I'll use the pictures that Adam took in that room and send them to your parents... our parents."

"AHHHH!" Zach yelled.

"I never wanted you to die, Zach. But this has to happen."

"No," Derrick's voice said from behind her in the darkness. "*This* has to happen."

Derrick squeezed the cinderblock so tight his knuckles were white. He slung it with all his strength he had in him.

Clunk. Evelyn's teeth jarred in her head and she flung to the ground in a dizzying pain. The gun dropped from her hand and fell to Kathrine. Evelyn couldn't see straight. She tried to fix her vision, and when she could finally see again, Natalie was standing over her.

She was holding a large shard of glass from the broken window and didn't care that it was cutting her palm. She reached down and jerked up the red hoodie to reveal the gunshot wound in Evelyn's side. "I wish I had better aim." She dropped to her knees and slammed the shard of glass into Evelyn's side right through the wound. Blood shot out onto Natalie's face.

"AHHHHH!" Evelyn yelled.

"No!" Natalie yelled at Kathrine. She was pointing the pistol and Evelyn's head. "Don't kill her," Natalie told her.

Derrick picked the cinderblock back up and stepped above Evelyn's legs. He aimed it right above her shins and dropped the cinderblock hard enough to break her legs.

Snap.

"She's not going anywhere..." Derrick said. Then, he pulled his phone from his pocket and hit play on the video on his screen. Evelyn's voice came from the phone. He recorded her entire confession.

Evelyn was gasping for air and holding her bleeding side.

"There you go," Natalie said as she dropped the ropes from around Zach's wrists.

Zach jumped up and ran to Kathrine.

"Baby, are you okay?" Zach asked.

Kathrine dropped the gun. "No... Everything is getting dark... I'm dizzy."

"We have to get her out of here!" Zach yelled at Natalie and Derrick.

"I've already called the cops. The ambulance will be here soon," Derrick said.

"Hold on, baby," Zach was desperate. "*Please*, hold on."

64

Derrick pulled his shirt over his head and balled it up. He pressed it against Kathrine's bleeding hip in hopes it would stop the weak fountain of blood.

"Don't do this," Zach cried. He was on his knees with Kathrine's bloody body in his lap. Her eyes were slowly opening and closing. Going in and out of focus. Zach's bushy beard and sparkling eyes were going from fuzzy to clear, then back to fuzzy.

Natalie was on her knees around her body, too. Derrick was still applying pressure to her hip. Evelyn was on the ground with her broken legs next to Adam's dead body. His eyes were open staring right at Evelyn.

"We're right here, Kathrine. You can make it," Natalie sounded just as desperate as Zach. She kept swinging her head to the door, hoping the cops would get there... soon.

"I love you, Kathrine. *I love you*. It's going to be okay," Zach's crying was getting louder.

Kathrine's breaths were getting more spaced out, and they were getting shallow. Her pulse was getting weaker and weaker. It was like the tides in the ocean shore. The waves came washing in earlier in the night, but not anymore. Now the tides were smaller, weaker. Until suddenly, the tide just simmered away and became a part of the sea. Silent. *Still.*

"Baby... look at me..."

She closed her eyes.

"*LOOK AT ME!*" he yelled.

Kathrine exhaled... and her body fell still. Her eyes didn't open again.

"Kathrine!" Zach yelled.

The blue police lights shined through the window.

"Kat! *Kat!*" Natalie yelled.

The cops ran in with their guns pulled. Sheriff Mullins led the way. Deputy Evans led the other cops into the different rooms of the house. Paramedics ran in; they squatted down at Evelyn's side, looking at her broken legs and the heavy cinderblock sitting on the shattered bones. Her legs were disgusting; blue and black all the way around, with blood oozing from the slices. The concrete dust from the cinderblock was sprinkled all over.

"Kathrine!" Zach yelled again.

Sheriff Mullins grabbed his radio and mumbled words into it that Derrick, Natalie, and Zach didn't hear. They were staring at Kathrine... holding on to what they had left. They stared at her chest, waiting for her heart to pump again. They stared at her mouth, waiting for her to take another breath. They stared at her eyes, waiting for them to open again... but they wouldn't.

She would never take another breath... she would never feel another heartbeat.

65

THREE MONTHS LATER

Evelyn went on trial the way she should have. She sat in her wheelchair next to her lawyer with the jury looking down at her. Derrick and Natalie sat behind her, and they were holding hands. The press was wanting information out of them, and they were getting it. They tried breaking Zach, but they never could. Zach was off the map... Derrick and Natalie hadn't heard from him since that night. They went to visit Kathrine, Jasper, and Genni's graves before graduation. They saw Zach standing at Kathrine's grave... and that was the last time they saw him. He didn't even walk at graduation.

Deputy Evans became Deputy Mullins. It was Fayetteville, so the speculation and opinions went crazy about their marriage. The sheriff married one of his deputies. The newspapers were having fun with that, too. On a national scale, the press was saying their relationship was unprofessional and let Evelyn and Adam run their gig as long as they did. It wasn't true, but it caused Sheriff Mullins to lose the reelection. But the thing was, he was okay with it. It upset Marie, but she was okay with it in time. She also turned in her badge and went to work for a hospital.

RED was finally done; there was no more murder and mystery haunting the back roads of that small, Tennessee town. But RED left a mark on Fayetteville. It was over, yes, but the terror lived on.

The sad thing was... it wasn't the worst thing that would happen to that town.

Dear reader,

Thank you so much for reading RED. It really means a lot to me. I grew up scared of letting anyone read my work. I was insecure and didn't think there was a purpose for anyone to read what I was writing. I published this online with a goal of having 10,000 reads in a year. I was SHOCKED to see the numbers... RED was read over 125,000 times in under 10 months.

You sparked a new inspiration in me. You pushed me to keep writing when I didn't want to anymore. You showed me there was a purpose to this. You kinda changed me... I hope you know that. And, I hope you know you can change other peoples' lives, too.

Your words have power.

There's too many "REDs" out there.

Love when it's hard.

Your friend,

Wes